The
Rooftop
Inventor

The Rooftop Inventor

The Adventures of
Theodocia Hews
Book 1

By NOOCE MILLER

Copyright © 2012 Nooce Miller

All rights reserved.

This book is a work of fiction. Names, characters, businesses, places, events and incidents are either the products of the author's imagination or used in a fictitious manner. Any resemblance to actual persons, living or dead, or actual events is purely coincidental.

No part of this book may be reproduced, or stored in a retrieval system, or transmitted in any form or by any means, electronic, mechanical, photocopying, recording or otherwise, without express written permission of the author except in the case of brief quotation embodied in critical articles and reviews.

Published by Caro Press, Indianapolis, Indiana.

ISBN: 1943380015
ISBN-13: 978-1-943380-01-5

Cover art by Melanie Berg.
Cover design by Camuffare Graphics.

First Edition, May 1, 2015.
Published in the United States of America

For my husband Guy, the great love of my life and my best friend. Exploring this magnificent world with you is the stuff of adventuring novels. More than anyone else, you made this book happen.

ACKNOWLEDGMENTS

I'm a big fan of fantasy fiction and I always have been. When the nifty little genre known as steampunk began to grow in popularity, I eagerly read as much as I could find. I especially enjoyed the works of two fantastic writers, Gail Carriger and Scott Westerfield. If you haven't read their books, I highly recommend you rush right out and get started on them.

And so the steampunk esthetic began growing in the back of my mind, taunting me with gorgeous mental images of altered Victorian reality. It occurred to me that almost all of the steampunk books I'd read were set in London or England, and I began daydreaming about a steampunk story set in my own neck of the woods, the American Midwest. After all, Cincinnati was a flourishing city back in the Victorian Era. Plus people always tell you to write about what you know, and although I've visited Great Britain, I can't say I know it very well. But I sure do know Ohio and Indiana.

I began imagining a teenaged heroine who wanted to be an inventor just like her father, but because society frowned on such a thing, she'd have to struggle between wanting to be a proper young lady to please her father and wanting to build things and fly airships and impulsively get into all kinds of ridiculous trouble. That's how Theodocia came to be. Right from the start, she was a handful. Smart, inventive, fearless, bossy, and most of all impulsive, she leaped fully formed upon the page and I knew I had something that would be really fun to write. And she hasn't let me down.

But just having an idea isn't enough. I'd like to thank those who made it possible for me to write this book.

First, my parents, who instilled in me a love of reading and writing. My mother never said no to a trip to the library or bookstore, and my father showed me that independent publishing was something I could do by first doing it himself.

Next I'd like to thank the Tuesday Writers' Group, for welcoming me into their fold. Rachelle, Alissa, Alice, Erin, Sam, and Andrea. Special thanks to Rachelle and Alissa (and Caitlin!) for being so wonderful when I met you at my first ever writers' convention and inviting me to join.

Huge thanks go out to my alpha reader—my sister Lisa—who gave me time she didn't have and took the first look. I'll never forget how exciting it was to read your comments and talk with you about my book.

Thanks also to my beta reader and fellow author Laurel Wanrow, who gave unstintingly of her time while she was working on publishing a book of her own. Laurel was amazingly helpful with her feedback, and it's been great fun for me to go through the process of writing and publishing a debut novel alongside her.

My cover artist, Melanie Berg, gave a visual form to Theo and then proceeded to create fantastic art for not one but three books. I am very grateful to have her beautiful images gracing my covers.

Last but of course not least, I'd like to thank my family. My husband Guy and our two sons Chris and Will waited with the utmost patience as I wrote my way through two other manuscripts (now sitting on the shelf) for this first book to come to fruition. I know *The Rooftop Inventor* wouldn't have been possible without their unflagging love, feedback, and encouragement.

CONTENTS

	Acknowledgments	i
1	Seen and Unseen	1
2	As Thick as Thieves	11
3	Without a Fighting Chance	27
4	Throwing Caution to the Wind	39
5	A Jumping off Point	49
6	Down on the Farm	59
7	In Hot Pursuit	73
8	Birds of a Feather	81
9	Dinner and Drama	89
10	Double Trouble	99
11	Shoot the Breeze	107
12	Set a Thief to Catch a Thief	113
13	Deeper in Trouble	119
14	What is Proper, and What is Right	127
15	The Lull Before the Storm	135
16	If the Truth Were Known	145
17	The Last Straw	155
18	Where There Is Smoke	165
19	On the Horns of a Dilemma	175

20	An Unexpected Outcome	185
21	Swallow My Pride	191
22	The Home Stretch	199
	Sneak Peek of The Voodoo Queen	207
	End Notes	211

CHAPTER 1

SEEN AND UNSEEN

"Charles, stop it. You can't follow me."

He looked up at me and tilted his little head as I climbed awkwardly onto the attic windowsill.

"You're being ridiculous. It's too high up," I said.

I turned away and started to push myself out of the window. I couldn't help myself, I looked back at him one last time. His eyes pleaded with me.

"Stop looking at me that way. You can't come out, it's too dangerous."

Since he is only a dog, Charles couldn't reply. When he was just a pup my father brought him back from a trip to London. I took one look at his beard and whiskers and named him Charles Dickens, but I think giving him such a dignified name has had the unwanted result of making him feel self-important.

He kept eyeing me suspiciously.

"Really, you should be used to this by now."

Emmoline, our housekeeper, hadn't heard me slip up the attic stairs, and Papa was out for the evening, so my luck was holding.

I turned my back on Charles, hitched up my skirts, and clambered from sill onto the roof because I needed to check on my aetherigible.

What is an aetherigible? Without meaning to boast, a lady never boasts, the aetherigible is a personal conveyance I am working on that shall revolutionize travel.

Everyone has seen the huge inflated airships floating lazily across the sky, carrying loads of pampered rich folks to and fro between cities like prize hogs traveling along in the back of a farm wagon. My invention is different. It's a small nimble airship that will allow one or two people to pilot themselves wherever and whenever they choose. Perhaps to the market, or to church on Sunday. Well, maybe not to church. I doubt the old ladies would be comfortable with a flock of aetherigibles bobbing around the steeple. Not dignified enough.

But for other errands, the aetherigible is an altogether more stylish option than walking or taking a horse drawn carriage. And it's much safer than riding those ridiculous high wheel bicycles when you live in a place as full of hills as Cincinnati.

Poised there just outside the attic window I wondered how I would look during my first flight. I already had a midnight blue flight jacket I received from Mrs. Titus, the seamstress, in exchange for a steam-powered sewing machine I refurbished for her. I also had a custom pair of brass-rimmed goggles polished up and ready to go. I hoped I would look like a proper airship pilot.

Moving cautiously on the slick shingles, I closed the window behind me so Charles wouldn't be tempted and then made my way up to the flat, hidden portion of the roof I use as my open-air workshop. I have to do my inventing in secret, because Papa doesn't approve of me tinkering around, especially after the time I tried to improve the heat output from our coal furnace with a steam powered fan and stained all our ceilings black.

Before I could so much as check a rope up there on the roof, the wind whipped and howled and blew a long flat chord on the chimney pots, and my skirt rose clear up around my waist, the hem snapping like a flag. If it had been daylight and if any of my neighbors had been outside in the tempest, they would have seen not only my petticoat but also the entirety of my white drawers, patches, mending, and all. I do wish I had some of the stylish new combination underthings to wear. Instead I wear my mother's old ones with the middle stitched up to modernize them, but it's best not to mention such things.

I yanked on my wayward skirt. I do strive so hard to be proper. 'Theo,' Papa always reminds me with great kindness, 'you must behave like a lady.' Though without a mother to show me how, I often find myself at a loss. Fighting to keep my lower anatomy covered, an important decision flashed through my mind. I must find a pair of trousers to wear while I work.

I'd just fitted the magenta envelope—that is, the pink silk cover that contains the lifting gas—onto the frame for the first time that morning, and now the wind was whipping it dangerously about. Magenta was the color I chose for the envelope instead of the usual tans and grays of most airships because when I finally do take to the skies, I intend to make a big impression. A little bit of showmanship helps you prove your point.

"Come on, get down off of there," I muttered to myself. The wind fought mightily with me as I released the brass buckles and dragged the soft, thin cloth down from the oblong frame, but I managed to gather it into my arms pretty quickly. I stowed the envelope inside the heavy tool box, closed the lid, and made sure the lightweight aetherigible platform and the empty frame were secured to the roof.

I paused a moment to run my hand down the cool metal rivets on the side of the upright black boiler. With my fingers I checked to be sure the curlicue of copper tubing that led from the steam chamber to the unusual second chamber protruding from the back side was firm. The brass collars were perfectly seated and the welds looked as good as any I'd ever seen come out of a machine shop. My original design featured an unusually small-sized firebox and boiler which allowed the steam engine to be light enough to be lifted by a small-sized envelope. And the curved legs kept the firebox away from the flammable platform below.

"Almost finished," I said. "Only a couple more parts".

Unhooking the propeller for a moment so it could spin free with the wind, I made a mental note to add a few drops of oil to the hub in the morning. I slowed the propeller blades and stopped them with the brake latch.

Satisfied the coming storm could do no damage, I looked out into the distance. Normally from my vantage point on the roof I could see all the way to the Ohio River, but tonight all I could make out were the ragged layers of clouds and the distant darkness that meant rain falling underneath. Then the clouds above my head filled with a bright flash of lightning. A prickling feeling began on the back of my neck. Thunder crashed, and with the wind tearing at my hair, I felt keenly alive.

I climbed back down into the attic where Charles sat anxiously whining.

"It's fine. Nothing blew loose."

He seemed pleased, and silently led the way out of the attic. I followed him down the stairs, but as he went on into the kitchen, I slipped out the side door and made my way into the alley. The wind roared in the treetops. No one saw me.

It was a Monday night, and I knew from long experience that Mrs. Goff four houses down could never prevail upon her many daughters to bring the wash in from the clothesline until Tuesday. And so as the rain began to pelt down on my head and shoulders, I cut between two carriage houses to the Goff's side yard. There hung three lines full of clothes, flapping in the gale and the sudden spatter of raindrops, most of them frilly girl's undergarments. With so many arrogant, fashionable daughters, it's a wonder Mr. Goff's laundry ever got any attention, but at last I found his things near the end of the third clothesline.

Luckily for me, Mr. Goff was a slender soul and his garments looked to be the right size. I pondered my choices. There hung Mr.

Goff's lounge trousers, a pair of his tweed breeches, and his dark, hand-tailored, best quality dinner trousers. The three pairs of pants waved cheerily at me, ankles up, all in a row.

"These are perfect." I smiled to myself.

The dinner trousers were my obvious choice. In addition to being a color that would effectively hide me while I climbed onto my hidden roof workshop at night, it delighted me to picture Mr. Goff *sans pantalon* amidst his large family of daughters at one of their remarkable dinner parties. Not that I've ever been invited for dinner. I've been to only one ball at their house and that was some time ago, but I understand the dinners are quite fashionable affairs.

I removed the pants from the line, taking care to replace the clothes pegs since I wanted to be sure Mrs. Goff noticed the loss. The rain was now slashing down in earnest, and it soaked me to the skin. Lightning was beginning to strike all around. For a moment I stopped to observe the branching white bolts up in the clouds. I do love a good storm.

Holding the trousers over my head in a futile attempt to keep my hair dry, I scurried back down the alley and burst in through our back door just as a huge bolt of lightning struck nearby, lighting up the night. The crash of thunder shook the house.

Charles jumped up on me as I used both hands to close the door on the storm, his dainty brown paws rending at my wet skirt as his tail lashed from side to side.

"Bad dog. Charles, you mustn't jump up. It isn't polite."

"Theodocia Hews. What have you gotten up to now?"

I yanked the sodden black pants off of my head. Quickly wadding them up, I thrust the bundle behind my back and whirled around.

Papa stood in the hallway, having just come in himself. His gray greatcoat was soaked from the waist down, and he wore a top hat with a dripping wet steel-ribbed black umbrella mounted on top. He took it off and glanced at its bent ribs in annoyance.

"I do wish you wouldn't alter my things without my permission. I was nearly laughed out of the Inventor's Society tonight when I walked in wearing it."

"Oh Papa, I forgot tonight was your meeting. Did you ask them about my application?"

"Theo—"

"Have they admitted me?"

"Theo…"

"I would be fine with an Apprentice Membership if they could just see their way to—"

"You may be even more persistent than your Uncle Adolphus is with the Abstractionist Assembly. I think that—"

"But my application is well founded," I interrupted. "And Uncle Adolphus is just jealous of the Abstractionists. If only—"

He held up his hand. "Theodocia Hews, my darling daughter, I told you, the Inventor's Society will not consider an application by anyone under the age of eighteen."

I drooped. "No, that's not it. The reason they won't admit me is because I'm a girl."

His mouth twisted up at one corner. "It might have more to do with the fact that no less than three times, you've interrupted meetings with your imaginative—er, demonstrations."

I'd forgotten all about that. Still, even though my most recent attempt—a kerosene powered stereoscope mini-engine—had caught fire and burned up the images the members had intended for that evening's presentation, the board still should have been impressed with the theory behind it. They'd known what to expect from me, the stereoscope engine was the third invention I'd tried to show them. I shook my head, driving out the stinging memory of their most recent rejection. I do so like to show people what I invent. If only they felt the same way.

"But Papa, what about the hat? Did it work? Did it keep you dry?"

"Not particularly well when the rain drove sideways. It also had a tendency to sail away in the wind." He looked at me, then gazed mournfully at his hat. "Theodocia, this was my only good hat."

"Sorry Papa."

I moved to slip out of the back hall and up the stairs, holding the pants down by my side, hoping they were hidden from sight in the folds of my skirt.

"Just a moment, young lady."

His words immobilized me. He put his hatbrella away on the polished walnut hall stand and took off his greatcoat.

A bit of a scare jolted through me, as Papa seemed to be on to me. But I'd been in this position too many times before to knuckle under. My mind darted as fast as a rabbit turns to avoid a cat in the garden, and an answer that would satisfy him appeared wholly formed in my mind. I pushed a tendril of dripping hair aside, and forced my eyes to meet his own. Show no fear. That is my motto.

He pointed to the pants then crossed his arms in front of his chest. "An explanation, if you please."

"I looked out the window upstairs. I saw these flapping in the storm, and I went outside to retrieve them."

All true, though not—strictly speaking—in that order. Papa says a lady must never tell a lie.

"We have spoken before—multiple times, I believe—about the inappropriateness of a young lady going about by herself outside after dark, have we not?"

"Yes, Papa." I hung my head.

"Somehow I think things were easier when you were younger and I could just take my paddle to your behind to make my point."

I smiled to myself, remembering the cushiony soft pillow paddle he'd invented to use when I was naughty. It never hurt one bit, because he'd never used it. Dear Papa never could stomach having to discipline me.

Papa sighed. "It's late. Go find Emmoline. When she's finished helping you undress and dry off, please ask her to bring me a pot of strong tea. I have a lot of work yet to do tonight. You can find out who those trousers belong to tomorrow."

"Yes, Papa." I murmured.

I kissed him on the cheek as I thought somewhat wickedly to myself, *but Papa, I already know—they belong to me.*

"Oh, and be sure to write that letter to your cousin Lettie."

"Papa, must I?" My vapid cousin Leticia Hews with her perfect blonde curls was not my idea of a fun summer visitor. She had a superior, citified air about her that set my teeth on edge every time we were together.

"With so little family left, Theo, we should not neglect the few we have. Get it done." He headed toward his study where he kept his plans, Charles padding along after him.

I knew Papa intended to get back to work on his most recent invention, the Hews Distance Vocalizer. His concept is that a person might speak into a curiously formed little box inside their house instead of sending a telegram or walking outside to holler at the neighbor across the fence.

Papa insists he's close to perfecting the technology, though I can't see how it could possibly improve on the gossip that already flies freely around our beloved Mount Belvedere neighborhood the same way it does all over town in spite of the steep pitch of the seven hills of Cincinnati. But perhaps I am somehow missing the point.

Poor Emmoline was less than pleased to see my sopping clothes and corset, and she raised an eyebrow at the black trousers, but she said nothing while she helped me undress.

She's been our housemaid my entire life, and she was my mother's family's housemaid before that. When we had to let our cook, the parlor maid, and the gardener go, I begged Papa to keep Emmoline. At her age she wouldn't be likely to find other employment, so she doesn't complain about little irregularities.

I'm seventeen now, and we all agree I am long past the age where I need a nursemaid. For a time when I was ten, I went for lessons at Woodward School on Sycamore Street downtown, but after I shocked the crowd of parents by quoting the entirety of Geoffrey Chaucer's *The Miller's Tale* at the Annual Examination, the headmaster paid me a great compliment when he told Papa there was not anything left for them to teach me.

I had a series of private tutors after that, and while my French did improve, they were no match for me. In spite of the generous pay offered by my father at the time, most broke down and tendered a tearful resignation by the second month. I count myself lucky Papa inherited his father's library. Not that Lettie or her brothers would have enjoyed the books. I have always set great store by book learning, and as books cannot talk back, they are my chief teachers and constant companions these days even if most of them are over fifty years old. Thank goodness we haven't been reduced to selling them. Yet.

"Those trousers will need to hang to dry," said Emmoline, her mouth set in a familiar straight line.

I wriggled into my nightgown and snatched up the trousers before she could take them. "Papa wants tea, if you please. I'll take care of these."

The dull brown housecoat she'd thrown on over her nightgown rustled as she walked past me to let herself out of my room. "Yes," she said drily, "I thought you would."

The innocent smile slid off of my face as she closed the door behind her.

Perhaps Emmoline isn't as unobservant as I thought.

CHAPTER 2

AS THICK AS THIEVES

The next day dawned bright and clear, and after Emmoline laced me up tightly and buttoned me into last year's walking dress, I began dreading the letter Papa had reminded me to write. Leticia Hews was my father's brother's only daughter. She had three older brothers who were all married and out on their own. By a quirk of fate, Lettie and I were one week apart in age, and so our fathers assumed we must be the best of chums.

Nothing could be further from the truth. Lettie and her mother were New York social climbers, and they constantly reminded me of the inadequacies of my "western" hometown of Cincinnati, which is silly when you consider how just about everyone here is trying to invent the next big steam powered machine and business is booming. But to hear them talk, you'd think we lived out on the open plains in patched canvas tents.

What's worse, they were enthusiastic believers in séances and spirit readings, which naturally anyone of any intelligence views as utter nonsense. The last time I'd visited them in New York, Aunt Eliza had insisted I come along to a spirit reading by one Mr. A. J.

Davis, which was to be held in a neighbor's parlor. Several other ladies were present, and they were all positively trembling with fear and excitement, Aunt Eliza and Cousin Lettie included.

First there was a lot of plaintive calling and moaning, and then Mr. Davis claimed the spirits were present and wanted to communicate with the living from across the divide. This was accomplished by his knocking on the underside of the table. I know because while everyone had their eyes closed, Mr. Davis included, I stuck my head under there and looked.

When I emerged from under the table his eyes flew open and he winked at me, so I held my tongue. But I knew he was a complete humbug, and after I caught him, I thought even less of the ladies who believed in him.

You see, I put my faith in science and engineering over their sham "spirit world." To my view, anyone who believes in ghosts or specters is a weak minded fool.

For all those reasons, I'd put off writing to invite Lettie to Cincinnati for over a month, but now Papa was asking with greater frequency and I knew I would have to get on with the job. I'd taken a trip to visit with them in New York last summer and now it was our turn to host Lettie. Papa says we must keep up appearances.

In my bedroom I keep a cunning little writing desk that once belonged to my grandmother. She gave it to me exhorting me to always keep up correspondences. Clearly, grandmother was far better at writing letters than I, as very few letters had ever issued from the desk during my ownership. I did write to the editors at The Scientific American from time to time, but I might as well have thrown those down a privy for all the response I got. Mostly I used my desk to write up notes on my various experiments, or to make entries in my diary.

Sighing, I sat down and pulled a few sheets of letter paper from the drawer. The thought of Lettie's dimples, her simpering mouth, and her haughty New York ways made me scowl savagely as I took up my pen.

My Dearest Cousin Leticia,

My father insisted that I write this letter to invite you for a visit. You know how important family is to me. Perhaps sometime next month would be agreeable to you. Why, just this morning I was remembering what fun we had frolicking at Fountain Square. Perhaps we can go there again! Please let us know if you are able to come to Cincinnati.

Kindest regards,

Theodocia

That ought to do the trick, I thought to myself, and I folded the letter and stuffed it into an envelope. When Lettie had last visited, we'd snuck away from the adults one afternoon. Once downtown, I managed to make her walk backwards so that she fell right into the icy fountain while I maintained plausible deniability. The letter should pass muster with Papa, who knew nothing of the incident, and yet it would express a clear message to my annoying cousin of what she could expect from another visit.

I put on my scuffed kid-leather button boots. Such sorry looking things they were. I positively craved a new pair. I traipsed downstairs into the dining room and kissed Papa good morning on his cheek, laying the envelope on the table in front of him. He looked worse for the wear after a late night in his workroom. I took his chin in my hand and tilted his face up to examine the dark circles underneath his eyes.

"Poor Papa, didn't you get any sleep at all?"

"None. I have until Friday to get the prototype and plans to Mr. Tamm, or else our contract is void." He rubbed his face and yawned.

Emmoline came in carrying a plate. She placed the fried eggs and bacon on the table and poured my father another cup of coffee. Her face looked more careworn than usual, and she hid a yawn with one hand.

"Papa, I was wondering, may I go buy a new pair of shoes sometime?"

He raised his reddened, bleary eyes up to gaze at my face. "Now Theo, you know we don't have money for new shoes right now. It pains me to tell you, but if I can't get the vocalizer finished this week, we will be looking for somewhere else to live. The bank doesn't look kindly on delayed mortgage payments."

That last bit shocked me a little. We'd been painfully low on funds for a few months, but I hadn't understood how dire our situation was. I wished I could help somehow.

While the vocalizer was well beyond my own ability, growing up with Papa had rendered me very capable in the realm of innovation, if only he would let me invent. How I longed to work at the high oaken bench by his side. If I could finish it, I knew my aetherigible could earn us piles of money, and if I were given untrammeled access to his workshop and his assistance, who knew what else I might be able to devise?

"Surely you're close to being finished. Is there anything I can do to help before I head over to Julia's?" I asked.

"Julia's? Oh my, I completely forgot about the Celebration. I'm sorry Theo, but we don't have any extra money for you to go downtown with Julia."

"But Papa, the hundred-year anniversary of John Jay and the Continental Congress signing Emancipation into law only comes around once."

"That's true, but I need your help today," he said.

I felt a little thrill run through me with those words. Suddenly, missing the Celebration seemed no big thing. How many times before had I declared my desire to help him, only to have him lecture me on how improper inventing was for a girl? Now, hard up against his deadline, he needed me. At last, I would stand by his side and use my expertise.

He rummaged around in his pockets then handed me a list and some money. "I'd like you to get me some things."

Shopping, not inventing. Clearing my throat to hide my disappointment, I tucked the folded paper into my pocket. I sighed quietly to myself, letting our old argument lay untouched where we had last left it.

"No breakfast?" He pointed at my place setting at the table.

"I'm going over to the Jepson's. I have to let them know I'm not going with them." I kissed his cheek again.

"All right, but please don't linger. I need that list filled, so head straight to the hardware store. And Theodocia, promise me, no extras on credit," he said pointedly.

I nodded and let myself out the front door, startling several robins pulling worms from the ground. They took off, skimming across the grass, chirping to one another. My unfashionably shod feet padded over the dew-covered lawn.

I looked at the flower borders as I made my way three doors down to the house of my best friend, Julia Jepson. The early summer roses were finished, but the orange day lilies and daisies were in beautiful bloom alongside mounds of pink petunias in Mrs. Prescott's borders. In the next yard a stand of crimson bee balm showed up brightly, industrious honeybees buzzing from bloom to bloom. As always, Mr. Banford's grass and hedges were neatly trimmed, bringing home to me just how shabby our own had become. My feet slowed. I dreaded having to tell Julia I couldn't join her today.

The third house from mine was Julia's, a lovely, tall, cream-colored house in the Queen Anne style.

"Good morning, Miss Theo." The Jepson's plump German-born housemaid gave me a warm smile as she let me in the front door.

"How do you do, Augustina?"

"Fine, thank you." She leaned in close to whisper in my ear. "Your papa's breakfast machine is working perfectly since you came over and adjusted it."

I raised my index finger to my lips. "Shhh, not a word. We wouldn't want his reputation to suffer. But you're welcome."

She smiled broadly. "Herr Doctor and family are at the morning breakfast table. Come with me."

She led me through the grand front hall past the door to Dr. Jepson's examination room, down the corridor that led to the dining room, and on into the glass-walled solarium on the east side of the large house. Bright sunshine streamed in through the glass paned ceiling and walls, showing off Dr. Jepson's prized collection of potted orange and lemon trees. The air was moist and warm. I breathed deep. The tangy smell of citrus tickled my nose.

"Good morning, Dr. Jepson. Hello Julia."

Dr. Jepson stood up politely as I came in. "Theo. Good morning."

Julia leaped up from her chair and gave me a quick hug. Jeremiah Junior, Julia's four-year-old brother, sat placidly squeezing a small rubber ball in one hand while he ate a piece of toast spread with jam with the other, his short legs swinging. When he saw me, he accidentally dropped the ball and it rolled under the table. I darted in, grabbed it, and gave it back to him before his father could say anything.

Little Jeremiah likes me in spite of the fact that I once attached mop heads to his hands and knees when he was a crawling baby as an experiment to see if he could clean the floor. Or maybe that's why he likes me. Hard to tell.

Julia has been my friend for as long as I can remember, and though she and her family enjoy high social status, she has never worried one whit about my ungovernable nature, like *some* girls do. Instead, she always appreciates my exploits. This particular morning she wore a brand new summer dress in a small floral print on a robin's egg blue ground. The dress set off her brown skin to perfection, and she wore her shining black hair up in a complicated pile of curls that was the latest style.

Julia and her mother enjoyed the daily services of their highly-trained New Orleans-born ladies' maid, Didiane, in addition to their housemaid Augustina and their cook, Susanne. Because of Didiane, Julia's French was better than mine. But only a little bit better. Certainly Julia's clothes looked better than mine.

I straightened the bold embroidered satin sash Julia wore over her shoulder so I could read it. "1779 – 1879, One Hundred Years of Emancipation," I read aloud. "I'm so sorry, Julia, but I won't be able to come with you. Papa needs me to run errands instead."

The smile fled Julia's face and her shoulders sagged a little. "Oh no, that's too bad."

With a rustle of silks, Mrs. Jepson came into the solarium. She too wore a colorful sash. "What's all this?" she asked in her soft, gentle voice.

"You were so kind to have invited me, Mrs. Jepson, but I'm afraid I can't go. Papa is rushing to finish his vocalizer and this morning I must go to the hardware store for him—again." I pulled the list out and waved it around, then put it back into my pocket.

Dr. Jepson folded the morning paper and put it down beside his plate. "I'm seeing patients this morning, but I'm going downtown afterwards. If you finish your errands and your father says yes, I could give you a ride."

"Thank you, that's a nice offer. I'll let you know what he says."

"Would you care to join us for breakfast?" asked Mrs. Jepson.

"No thank you. I'd best get going. Papa has contract terms to meet."

Julia walked me to the door. "Please finish as fast as you can," she said.

"I will, I promise," I said. "I need to tell you what happened last night."

She gave me a quick hug, and I walked out the door.

Visions of my aetherigible floated in the air before me as I made my way on foot down the hill. How it would speed my errands if only I could fly. Normally, I take the incline car and sit gazing out at the splendid panoramic view of downtown and the winding river from the heights of North Elm Street. But the car was at the bottom, loading passengers, and I had no time to wait for it to slowly grind its way back up to the top of the hill.

I kept up a brisk pace and in spite of my efforts to be a dutiful and helpful daughter, all I could think of was what I still needed to get my aetherigible flying. With this trip to the store, I should be able to purchase the last few items necessary to get my compressor working. And with one more pressure gauge, I would finally be able to fill the waxed silk envelope with the substance I had discovered through my own experiments. I had named the lighter-than-aether gas *nyx*.

I reached into my pocket to touch the coin purse there. A strong wave of guilt washed over me as I remembered my father's words. No extras. I had no money of my own, only what he'd given me. Of course, his inventions paid our bills, and a good daughter always minds her father. This time I would not be adding an expensive gauge nor anything else to the list.

I tried to conjure up a mental picture of the vocalizer. Only three inches to a side, the ebonized wooden case was packed with novel instrumentation and covered with brass switches and knobs with an open hole on one face. When I had carried Papa's lunch out to him in his workshop behind the house the day before, he had the thing taken completely apart and the pieces laid out on his workbench. No doubt he'd been tinkering with some final improvement, which I supposed was why I had been sent out for parts today.

Many businessmen had shown great interest in this newest contraption of his right from the start. Before he'd settled on terms with Mr. Tamm, there'd been a host of other attentive suitors. The most memorable among them had been that ridiculous set of French-born twins in striped skirts and tight bodices who came to visit Papa. They'd been sent by their employer, a Mr. Hiram Quigley from Chicago. These two young women had received such gifts from nature, it would make a minister blush to look at them. Clearly they planned to use their beauty to increase their influence with Papa, as is often the case with women who look like that.

If he would only sell them full rights to the vocalizer, they promised to also give him the second production model of some sort of racing steam carriage their employer had paid to have manufactured in Dayton. But steam powered carriage or no, Papa did not find their terms to his liking, and feminine charms notwithstanding, I was glad when he declined.

That had been months ago, but then we'd seen them on the street downtown again just the other day, alighting from a carriage right in front of us. They wore shiny silk dresses in the French style. Two identical sets of powdered cleavage prominently and oh-so-inappropriately displayed. Their ugly driver didn't so much as lift a finger to help them. Papa nearly dropped his packages when he leaped beside their carriage to offer his hand.

I cannot abide a woman who willfully flirts, and there stood two of that sort, smiling and whispering in Papa's ears the same way they'd done the time before. He was so caught up in his discourse with them, I could scarcely catch his attention to remind him of our urgent appointments in town. When I learned later they had not persuaded him to go back on his deal with Mr. Tamm, it came as a considerable relief.

Mr. Tamm was expecting to file for the patent on Papa's device just as soon as my father finished it. Several other inventors out east were working on devices to transmit a human voice, but Papa's was wireless, and so Mr. Tamm thought he would have the business advantage over any others.

Papa expected me to go to Gordon's Hardware & Dry Goods, but on a whim, I detoured to Findlay Market on West Elder Street on the off chance I might be able to find the items he must have for a lower price, freeing up a little money for my own needs. Findlay Market was one of my favorite haunts, and I often ran errands there for Emmoline. I knew where to buy the best and cheapest produce, and I knew which junk vendors could be trusted and which ones to avoid.

The market was buzzing with activity and my mood picked up. I greeted some of my favorites as I made my way through the crowd past their stalls—Mr. Dauffel the butcher, Miss Tandy the greengrocer who had fresh vegetables to sell even when it was winter, and the Crane brothers who sold poultry—but I didn't stop, because I was headed to see an old friend of mine. I doubt that very many housewives were ironing this Tuesday, because it seemed to me that all of them were at the market, juggling their packages and hefting chubby-faced babies from one hip to the other, enjoying the summer day.

As I made my way past the crowd, I felt fingers grip then release my upper arm. A short, stout woman wearing a colorful head wrap and dangling earrings stood close behind me, clasping both her hands together with a look of astonishment on her face.

Another spirit charlatan. I'd stop her before she could get her pitch out. "No thank you. I don't want a spirit reading."

"You...you..." she stuttered.

"No thank you," I said, louder this time.

"The door is nearly open," she said, her nervous eyes darting to look around the market then back to my face.

"Door? What a lot of pig swill. Go find some other mark to pester. I have errands to run."

Her face looked stricken and her mouth worked soundlessly. She stumbled backwards without speaking again.

I confess, I was a little curt with her. Maybe the fact I couldn't buy the shoes I needed made me cranky. Or maybe the woman brought to mind my cousin Lettie and Aunt Eliza and all of their ghostly trance clap-trap, irritating me. I should have been polite, but the woman had laid hands on me without the least invitation. My good manners have been known to fail when I am provoked.

I wouldn't let a trifle spoil my day. I turned and wove my way through the stalls of farm produce. Fresh vegetables in every color of the rainbow lay heaped in bushel baskets on the ground or arranged on temporary tables. Lettuces, radishes, peas in the pod and newly dug baby beets shouldered for space against strawberries, and in the place of honor, a pile of pale green Thompson grapes.

As I reached the section of the market where the bakery was housed, the homely smell of warm bread wafted through the air, and my mouth began to water. I regretted my decision to skip not one but two breakfasts.

I moved closer, and the sweet smell of cakes baking drifted into my nostrils. My feet simply stopped at the bakery and then joined the line of their own volition. I insist I had not one iota of control over them at that moment.

An attractive young man casually leaned against the corner post holding up the bakery's white canvas awning. He was looking straight at me in a most impolitely familiar way, though we were not acquainted. I noticed him not because his face was handsome or his eyes were a sparkling shade of blue, nor yet because he was wearing a rather shabby coat. And it wasn't that his thick, wavy, dark brown hair was without benefit of a hat, which made him seem even more out of place amongst the great tide of female shoppers as he gazed levelly at me. Instead, I noticed him because of what came next.

Tapping my toe, I stood in line behind a young German woman who had sent the baker inside to fetch a loaf of rye. I was contemplating whether to ask the baker for apple fritters or angel cake, when all of a sudden, the handsome young man darted around the table. He shot another bold look straight into my eyes, causing my mouth to drop open, then he seized the largest loaf of bread from the middle of the table and took off running.

"Polizei!" shouted the startled housefrau. Hearing her cry, the baker ran back out and frantically began counting the loaves on his table.

Spotting an officer of the law nearby, I added my own English-speaking voice to the din, thinking it might have some positive effect. "Police! Stop! Thief!"

Pulling his wooden billy club from his belt, the policeman leisurely strolled over toward us, to all appearances oblivious to the thief fleeing past him.

"What seems to be the problem, madam?" He stroked his thick black moustache, speaking to the housefrau.

"Deef, deef! Th—th—thief!" sputtered the housefrau.

I cleared my throat. "A young man in a worn black coat without a hat has stolen a large loaf of bread. He ran that way." I pointed down Elder Street, but the police man only looked me up and down.

"Run, man!" shouted the baker. "Catch him!"

The policeman drew himself up, raising his chin and straightening his collarless navy blue police waistcoat. He fixed his gaze on my front, then slowly raised it to look me in the eye. "I would have to see the thief in order to give chase."

It angered me he was ogling instead of doing his job. Looking at his well-rounded stomach, I spoke my mind, another fault for which I am well-known. "Why, you didn't even bother to look in the direction we pointed while he made his escape. I should think you would be ashamed. You are a poor excuse for a policeman." I noticed his brass buttons lacked shine. "And your buttons could use some elbow grease."

"Move along," the policeman growled, and he walked away without helping.

About that time I noticed the baker—in a most unwarranted way—had shifted his angry visage to me as though I were the cause of the policeman shirking his duties, and I decided I had best continue on without breakfast.

I walked on to the area where dry goods and used items were sold. This was my favorite place in all of Findlay Market. On Tuesdays and Saturdays, upon wagons, upon rickety tables, upon tatty blankets laid directly on the dusty road, the sellers placed the most astonishing assortment of bits and bobs, wires and metal gewgaws, thingamajigs and gadgets imaginable—all of unknown provenance.

Several of the men said hello as I wove my way through their tables and piles. I greeted each one in turn, heading straight past them to where a red wool blanket with ragged edges and holes lay flat on the ground. As I approached from one side, I spotted the proprietor, a man wearing a one piece, dun-colored coverall, standing behind a tall boiler. He handed a brass cylinder over to his customer, who dropped a coin into his palm, thanked him, and walked away. Then the vendor looked up and catching sight of me, he smiled and waved, displaying a wide open space between his two front teeth and a thick rim of black grease under each fingernail. If I had any chance of finding the items on Papa's list and still having a little money left over, it would be here.

"Good morning Mr. Crenshaw."

He pulled his cap from his head and nodded once. "Miss Theo. I wondered if you'd be coming 'round the market today."

"Wouldn't miss it." I pulled the list from my pocket and paused, reading it over then peering into his boxes.

"Now then, what will you be needing?" asked Mr. Crenshaw.

As I mentioned before, Mr. Crenshaw was an old friend. He'd been a great help in finding the pieces I'd needed to build the steam engine for the aetherigible. His goods lay on the red blanket in a ragtag assortment of wooden boxes and rusty metal lids, and from my past experience buying from him, I knew him to be an honest man.

Well, honest except for that small matter of unknown provenance, which I tried not to think about.

"Papa sent me to fill this list," I said, handing the paper over.

Mr. Crenshaw's mouth worked as he made out each word. Then he handed the list back. "I reckon I have everything but the number twenty-five measure copper wire. I'm afraid you'll have to visit Gordon's for that."

He began sorting through his boxes, bins, and piles, pausing every now and then to select an item which he then placed onto a stack of dirty newsprint. How he knew precisely what lay underneath each heap of junk was a mystery to me.

He'd just moved some glass jars out of a crate to find the last item on the list when a golden gleam caught my eye. I held my breath as I beheld a beautiful, calibrated, 300-psi gauge with a glass-fronted one-and-one-half inch dial. It wasn't new, but it had been freshly polished. What was more, right beside it lay my Holy Grail, a brass-mounted altimeter with a three-inch dial. Not strictly necessary for flight, but it would sure come in handy.

"See something you like?" he asked casually, knowing full well I'd been hunting a 300 psi gauge for over a month.

"How much?" I tried to keep my voice even.

"Forty cents," he said. He picked up the smaller brass beauty and rubbed the glass gently with his sleeve.

I gulped. Rice and beans cost around 10 cents per pound. We could eat for weeks for the price of that gauge. Not well, but Emmoline said rice and beans made good nourishment for a body. My face flushed red with shame, thinking of how I'd blithely nodded my promise to Papa only a short time before. *No extras.*

"What do I owe you for the list items?"

He scratched his chin while he ciphered in his head. "Four and eleven, that's fifteen cents total."

I pulled out my coin purse and sorted through the little money I had, frowning.

Mr. Crenshaw smiled and tilted his head. "Too rich for your blood?"

I could not even bargain with him. The gauge was beyond my means. And the altimeter was only a dream. I had seventeen Indian head pennies and two nickels in my purse.

"I might be able to make you a better deal. Let's say, twenty-five cents including the gauge, and you'll bring me one of those nice rhubarb pies Missus Mills makes."

He knew good and well that Emmoline would never give me a pie with the price of sugar so dear. I would have to steal it, but it wouldn't be the first time a pie had gone missing, and I knew he would tell no one.

I hesitated, thinking of what Papa had sent me out to do. That ten cents should be spent elsewhere. My fingers itched to touch the smooth brass.

"If you could bring me a peck of them cherries that are coming on in your backyard orchard, I could throw in the altimeter," he said with a wink and a smile. "You'll still have two cents left over to go get that wire."

My heart sang in my chest at his kindness. "Oh, Mr. Crenshaw!"

He lifted the altimeter up and held it out to me. "Just look at it. Ain't it pretty?"

I took it and turned it this way and that in the sunlight to admire it before handing it back.

"Done. But please wrap the gauges separately. We don't want to worry Papa."

Mr. Crenshaw wrapped my items in old newsprint, tying them up carefully with a length of string. He bundled up Papa's items, then held out his hand for the money. "Fly by and see me when she's airworthy," he said, smiling his gap-toothed smile.

CHAPTER 3

WITHOUT A FIGHTING CHANCE

I almost—but not quite—skipped toward Gordon's to get the wire. I would have done so had such footloose behavior not been unseemly for a young lady of my age and social standing. It must be confessed that I might possibly have skipped for a couple of steps on Race Street as I turned the corner to go north up Vine back to the house, but only because I needed to get out of the way of a large draft horse pulling a cart.

Before long I made my breathless way back up the steep hill to our house on Mount Belvedere. The late morning sun was already hot and sultry, and I kept to the shade as I took the shortcut up the alley. The cicadas were singing the way they do in mid-July. When I reached our backyard, I noticed the door to the barn Papa uses as his workshop was open, but I didn't see my father sitting inside on his high stool so I continued on to the house.

In retrospect, I should have noticed something was wrong. Papa never left the door to his workshop open to prying eyes, and a trash bin was overturned by the back fence. But I didn't think anything of it at that moment, so I went inside the house. I didn't see my father in his study. Emmoline, who was in the kitchen ironing Papa's shirts, didn't know where he was, so after I'd hidden the paper-wrapped gauges in my room I went back out to his workshop, intending to leave the items he'd asked me to fetch on his bench.

A horrible sight met my eyes.

Papa lay sprawled on the floor, his stool overturned, and a small puddle of blood on the brick pavers by his head.

"Papa! Papa?"

I dropped to my knees and shook him gently to wake him, but he did not move. A sickening twinge began at the back of my head then spread downwards until it lay twisting and quivering nastily in the pit of my stomach.

"Emmoline, come quickly. Emmoline!" I shouted at the top of my lungs. I heard the faint squeak of the kitchen door from across the lawn and then she was with me.

"What on earth?" Emmoline's face turned very pale when she saw the blood.

"Emmoline," I said, striving to keep my voice calm, "My father's hurt. You must fetch Dr. Jepson. Run!"

Had I taken too long at the market? Had the doctor already locked up and departed?

"Papa, wake up."

He didn't stir.

I took out my handkerchief and tried to press it to the back of his head without moving him too much. I couldn't tell where the blood was coming from, so I left the handkerchief where it was and held his hand instead.

"Papa?"

He lay motionless. Hot tears filled my eyes but I rubbed them away and clenched my teeth together instead. I've never thought much of girls who weep in difficult situations, and it angered me to think I'd almost let myself become one of them. I pressed my lips together and set to rolling up my sleeves. I felt marginally calmer, but not much. The terrible twisting down in my midsection was still there.

I could hear the sound of a redbird calling boldly over and over again up in the top of the tallest tree in our yard, and I wished it would stop.

Where were they? They were taking forever.

I put the back of my hand in front of Papa's nose to try to feel for his breath. For several awful moments, I didn't think there was any air moving. I tensed, my own heart pounding loudly in my ears.

I held very still and finally I could feel the tiny puff of air on my fingers. He still lived.

"They're in here," I heard Emmoline say at last, and then the two of them were in the doorway.

Dr. Jepson took one quick look and he dropped his bag on the cobblestone floor and began searching for a pulse in Papa's neck. The doctor's sure hands moved fluidly over his patient while his face and shoulders grew rigid with tension.

Emmoline stood helplessly in the doorway twisting the hem of her apron in her hands. I wrapped my arms around my body and held my breath.

Dr. Jepson relaxed and took his hand away. "His pulse is thready but his heart is still beating. Was he like this when you found him?" he asked.

"Yes. I didn't move him. He won't wake up," I said.

Slowly, carefully, the doctor turned Papa's head to one side and then gingerly felt the back of his skull with the tips of his fingers.

"He's taken a nasty blow to the back of his head, but I don't think his skull is broken." Dr. Jepson shot a look at me, then back toward the doorway. "Emmoline, go find a man to help me move him inside."

"I think Mr. Banford's gardener works on Tuesdays," she said, her voice quavering, and she whisked out the door.

I darted to the back corner of the workshop where my father kept a stack of leftover lumber and began going through the pieces until I found a wide plank that was just over six feet long. I pulled it out and carried it over to where Dr. Jepson was kneeling on the ground.

"You can use this to carry him." I laid the plank alongside Papa. "I'll help you get him onto it."

Dr. Jepson quickly took his fingers away from Papa's face where he'd been prying one eyelid open. He looked up at my skinny arms and thin waist and hesitated.

"I'm stronger than I look."

"All right. Take his legs and I'll get his shoulders."

With one swift motion, we had him on the board. Papa still didn't stir or speak.

Emmoline returned with a large man wearing muddy boots.

"What happened?" the man asked. "Did he fall off that?" He gestured at the tall stool lying off to the side.

Irritation flashed through me. "No. Someone's attacked my father. Emmoline, please go fetch the police."

I carried Dr. Jepson's bag, held the doors open, and kept Charles out of the way while the men maneuvered their way into the house and up the stairs with the makeshift stretcher. I even thought to grab a plush cotton towel from the washstand to cover Papa's pillow before they laid him onto his bed. The gardener stood back, suspiciously eyeing Papa's bedside clock with its jointed wake-up arm. His eyes grew wide as he took in the eerily realistic hand-shaped writing automaton perched on Papa's desk.

Dr. Jepson poured some water from the ewer into the bowl and began using a small facecloth to dab at the blood.

I stood watching helplessly, wishing there was something I could do. The gardener edged toward the door. Papa's room seemed oddly small and crowded with the two men moving around in it.

Dr. Jepson began rooting around in his doctor's bag, so I showed the gardener down the stairs and out the back door. By then Emmoline had returned with not one but three police officers, Captain Van der Pool and two others.

I hadn't really wanted to call for them, but it couldn't be helped. The Captain and the rest of the officers know me well after the gaslight incident. One time a few years ago I'd tried to invent a street heater to allow people to wait for a hansom cab in comfort during winter. My faulty plumbing caused all the gaslights on our street to explode one after the other. And there've been other minor happenings when I came into contact with the police—too numerous to mention now. The police are always polite to me, and Papa says Captain Van der Pool is even rather fond of me, but suffice it to say I usually try to steer clear of them. But with Papa's injury there was nothing for it, I needed their help.

"Now what's the trouble here?" said the Captain, following me out the door, across the yard, and into the workshop.

"Someone entered my father's workshop through this door here," I said, gesturing with my hands, "crept up behind him over here where he was working, and struck him on the head with a heavy club."

Captain Van der Pool looked down at the darkening blood and crossed his arms. "Where is he?"

"How would I know? He's run away I suppose."

"Your father ran away?"

"No," I said crossly, "whoever hit him ran away."

"Where's your father?"

"Dr. Jepson took him into the house."

"Well then we'll just go inside and speak with him."

"You can't. He's unconscious."

One of the patrolmen picked up the high stool and put it back in its place in front of the workbench.

"Wait, isn't that evidence of the crime?" I said.

"This?" He looked back at me blankly, one hand on the stool. "Did you see the man hit him with it?"

"No, I wasn't here."

"Well then, how do you know someone hit him?"

Captain Van der Pool crossed the room to examine the stool. "He has a point. How do you know your father didn't just fall over backwards?"

I could feel the pressure rising in my temples, and I rubbed my head with my fingertips.

"Because he always works at that bench sitting on that stool, and he's never fallen before," I snapped.

"Always a first time," said the other officer.

They began to move toward the door to go to the house. I clutched at the Captain's sleeve.

"Wait. Aren't you going to look around? Perhaps someone's stolen something." I quickly scanned along the parts and half-built contraptions with my eyes. Papa's workbench was chockfull of its usual assortment of hand tools, machined metal parts, gears, cogs, copper tubing, nuts, bolts, and various assemblages, but it all felt off to me somehow.

"I thought this was supposed to be an assault," said the Captain. "Now you're saying it's a robbery?" He walked back over to where I stood and looked along the cluttered surface, picking up the fancy front piece from an ormolu clock and turning it over in his hands, then replacing it. "Uh, exactly how are we to know if something's missing?"

"There are valuable metals there," I said, pointing.

Strangely enough, none of the small apothecary-style drawers in the little cabinet at the end of the bench had been disturbed. I strode over to reach for the pulls, and when I opened it, all the small coils of wires made from precious metals were still there, intact.

"Hm, looks fine to me," the Captain said.

But I still had the strong feeling that something wasn't right. The spot in front of the stool was conspicuously empty, and I felt a dizzying rush as I realized what looked wrong to me. The prototype Distance Vocalizer and Receiver set was missing, as were Papa's hand drawn plans for its manufacture.

"The Vocalizer is missing, and the receiving part too."

"The Vo-what?" said the first officer.

"It's—his invention," I said, holding my hands out and shrugging helplessly. I couldn't begin to explain what it was, not to them.

The second officer sidled up to me and put his large hand on my shoulder. "Now don't you fret, miss." He gave me a couple of pats and they began to move toward the door again.

My face began getting hot. "Wait! You need to do a proper job here first!"

The tiny corner of something white stuck out from underneath a wooden crate below the bench, catching my eye. Using my fingernail, I dragged it out.

I'd found an airship ticket from Chicago to Cincinnati. It had been stamped as cancelled on Friday, four days ago. I quickly read it to myself.

Passenger: Salarnier, Angelique, Miss.

The notation at the bottom showed it had been purchased by none other than Hiram Quigley of Quigley Enterprises, West Madison Street, Chicago. Mr. Quigley. The businessman who sent the Salarnier twins to try to strike a deal not once but twice. Someone who wanted the vocalizer very badly. The realization of who had attacked my father suddenly came to me, and red hot anger boiled up.

"This is the culprit," I said, handing the ticket over to the nearest policeman, who took it from me.

The others drew close and bent their heads to look at the ticket.

The Captain was the first to meet my eyes. "The date is from four days ago, not today. And this is a lady's name. A lady wouldn't hit a man. There's nothing to suggest any connection to what's happened here."

"But—But—" I sputtered. "They had a driver. An ugly man."

"Now, now, it doesn't do to jump to conclusions. Let us do the police work. It's time we went in to see your father. We can take another look around out here later."

I showed them inside, but it took all the self-control I had not to tell them off.

A little while later, after the policemen had established for themselves that my father was indeed unconscious and couldn't tell them what had happened, they went back outside to take another look around the yard, and then they left to search the neighborhood.

I stood in the kitchen a moment comforting Emmoline, who was wiping her eyes with the corner of her apron. I was just about to go back upstairs when Dr. Jepson came down. He stood before us in the kitchen, his face grave.

"How is he?" I asked.

"Your father has suffered a severe blow to the back of his head. I've done all I can do for now, but there is some risk of bleeding on the brain and I will have to stay with him to watch over him."

Emmoline hid her face in her apron and wept.

"The policemen wouldn't listen to me when I told them someone hit him," I said.

"You did fine. I told them I thought from the wound someone struck him with a heavy object. Why don't you go outside and get some air for a moment and I'll go back up."

This was a good idea, because I needed to think. I wandered around the yard where the police had tramped all around the grass in their heavy boots. My thoughts circled around and around, but I always came back to the same thing.

In the end, I didn't stop to tell Dr. Jepson or Emmoline where I was going, because I knew they would try to talk me out of it.

I had no choice. I had to get that vocalizer back before Friday. If I didn't, we would lose the house, all its contents, and even the bed in which my injured father lay. I felt anew the shame of disobeying my father's wishes that morning, and I knew if he were awake, he would not approve of my course of action, but this was important. Dr. Jepson would take care of him while I was gone.

I was certain the twins' ugly henchman had assaulted my father and they'd taken the vocalizer. I figured the racing steam carriage—the one the twins had talked about when they'd made their offer to my father earlier on—had finally been delivered to them. Though I didn't know its top speed, I suspected it could move more swiftly than a locomotive since it must be much lighter in weight. The only way I could possibly reach Chicago before they did would be to get aboard the fastest airship in the fleet. The Peregrine, the only ship of its class in the entire Midwest and the pride of its line, made the direct Cincinnati to Chicago run on Tuesdays. With its propeller set at full power it had a top speed of 35 miles-per-hour in favorable winds, so it would reach Chicago tonight.

My only other option was a passenger locomotive which traveled at top speeds of 40 miles-per-hour, but with constant stops at every small town along the route to take on and discharge passengers and freight, I knew I would never make it in time by train.

I had to take the Peregrine.

Without so much as putting on my hat, I ran into the workshop and grabbed a handful of gold and silver wire and ran pell-mell down our hill and up the next, winding through the streets to the airship terminal.

Breathless, I dashed into the building and up to a ticket window and slapped down my crumpled handful of wire.

"I'm sorry miss, what is this?" The station agent picked up the tangled mess and examined it.

"Gold. And silver, I think. Or maybe platinum." I paused and gasped for air. "A one-way ticket on the Peregrine, destination Chicago. Next flight out, if you please."

The agent looked down his nose through his spectacles at the wire coils in his hand, then looked back up at me. "I will need to clear it with the station manager first, miss. And, hm—maybe find a scale." An inch at a time, the large man raised himself up from his padded stool and waddled into the back room.

I drummed my fingernails impatiently on the high wooden counter, making such a racket that the woman and man at the next window looked at me sidelong then picked up their luggage and moved farther away to the last agent in the row.

"Come on. Come on," I whispered under my breath, curling my fingers into a fist. My breath went in and out in quick little puffs.

After a long time, during which I thought I might lose my mind, the agent returned, trailing his superior. The manager wore an expensive three-piece suit in the latest style, with a thick gold watch chain stretched across his chest.

"You wish to purchase a ticket."

"Yes. And quickly."

"With...this?" he said, and he thrust out my handful of wire coils.

"Those wires are drawn gold. And silver."

"Or platinum. She thinks," said the agent.

The manager turned his sizeable nose up into the air, and brought all of his authority to bear on me. "I beg pardon, miss. But we are unable to accept *wire* in the place of currency. The ticket costs one-hundred fifteen dollars. I apologize for the inconvenience, but you will need to convert this—*ahem*—gold to dollars at a bank."

He dropped the crumpled wires onto the counter, spun on his heel, and strode away.

"How long do I have?" I said to the agent.

"Why, you can take as long as you like, miss."

"No, you great fool, how long until the Peregrine takes off?"

The agent fiddled with some papers in front of him to check the schedule, frowning. "Four days."

"Four days? But isn't there a voyage today?"

"Yes miss, but it left before you got here."

Enraged, I shrieked right in the man's face, startling him considerably. I snatched up my gold and raced back toward home. There was only one thing for me to do.

CHAPTER 4

THROWING CAUTION TO THE WIND

The sun was high in the sky by the time I arrived back home. Dejected but not yet entirely daunted, I let myself in the back door. Emmoline was nowhere in sight, so I rushed up the stairs to check on Papa. Dr. Jepson had not moved from his place at the bedside. Faithful Charles lay on the coverlet at Papa's feet. His nose twitched and his eyes followed me as I came in, but he stayed where he was.

"Has he woken up at all?"

Dr. Jepson shook his head. He took up his stethoscope and pressed it to Papa's chest. "Still not as steady as I would like. I believe there is dropsy of the brain from the force of the blow. This will be a dangerous night for him."

The queasy flutter in my stomach returned. I stepped close to the other side of the bed and took up Papa's hand.

Dr. Jepson put his stethoscope back down on the nightstand and sat back in his chair. His expression was gentle. "You have blood on your sleeve and skirt. Why don't you go to your room to change out of your dress and try to get some rest, my dear?"

I looked down in some surprise. No wonder the people at the Airship Station had looked so oddly at me.

"Where is Emmoline?"

"She was in hysterics, so I sent her over to my house. Augustine is no doubt plying her with a soothing chamomile tea. Can you manage without her?"

"Yes, of course. It's just ..." I looked down helplessly at Papa.

"I won't leave him. Go ahead. He's stable enough for now."

Feeling great reluctance, I placed Papa's hand back onto the coverlet and patted it. I kissed his cool cheek.

Without looking back, I closed the door behind me and paced down the hallway, my eyes burning.

In my own room, I pulled off my bloodstained dress and cast it aside, popping several buttons in the process. I was awash in several strong and opposing emotions. Earlier, I had harbored great anger that someone had injured dear Papa in such a terrible way. That anger had carried me down the hill and up the next, through my failed attempt to board the Peregrine, and back home again. But now that I had seen Papa lying insensible in his bed, I found myself overwhelmed by another sensation, one wholly foreign to me. My lips and chin trembled, my legs felt wobbly, and I had a hard time breathing. If I had been a weaker young woman, uncontrollable whimpering might have resulted.

I struck the tears away from my eyes with my hands. I have always prided myself on being a logical, thinking person. Wallowing in fear or self-pity would change nothing. I knew I needed to *act*, and quickly, but what should I do?

The door of my wardrobe swung open in my hand, and some of the pieces of my time machine caught my eye. If only I could go back in time and warn Papa not to go into his workshop. But my time machine was not yet finished, and I had no companion anchor machine in the workshop to which I could send myself anyway.

I took out a dark red travel dress with a ruffled skirt and put it on, trying to make up my mind.

I sat down at my writing desk and began a note to Papa in a quick running hand. Penmanship has never been one of my talents, and I fear my emotions at that moment were getting the better of me. My words were not very legible.

I was struggling to write what I was thinking when the same weakness and black smothering sensation struck me again. I sat back in my chair and closed my eyes. In that dark moment I entertained the notion that all was lost, and that I ought to just stay at home by Papa's side and try to do something useful, like darning Papa's stockings. But this surrender to feminine softness quickly passed. Such is not my character.

Before long I found my eyes wandering around the room, and when they rested upon the small package wrapped in dirty newsprint and tied up in string, my strength returned and I knew what I had to do.

"Oh Papa, I do hope you will understand."

I bent over the desk and finished the letter. Signing it with a flourish, I left it lying on the desk. With a new, single-minded focus I yanked my tailored, tight-fitting jacket and goggles from the wardrobe. Pulling them on, I strode from the room.

My first stop was the library downstairs, where I snatched up maps of Ohio, Indiana, and Illinois. A glance at a distance table showed Chicago lay nearly 295 miles from Cincinnati, allowing for a stop in Indianapolis for supplies.

I also took up a blank journal and an ink pen I found there. Next was Papa's workshop, where I borrowed his small toolbox. A pilot needs to be able to conduct repairs on the fly. I reentered the house and stood for a moment at the bottom of the back stairs. All was still. I doubted Augustine had left off her ministrations of her friend and sister-housemaid as yet.

Squaring my shoulders, I strode with purpose up the stairs, into the attic, and out onto the roof. Not much daylight remained. Though the day had seemed endlessly long at times, the sun was almost at the horizon. I got to work.

I'd completed the platform of the aetherigible some time ago. While wicker is lightweight, bamboo is stronger, and so by means of several nighttime tours of the City Arboretum Greenhouse, I had harvested enough bamboo to lash together the base and sides. I checked it over, and found to my satisfaction that months of exposure on the roof had not weakened its design. The little seat I had built in behind the controls was still tightly fixed to the floor. I stowed my maps in the tight little box I had installed for that very purpose, and opened up Papa's toolbox.

My next task was to check over and tighten the oblong framework with a wrench and then to apply the rubberized silk. The buoyancy of an airship is dependent upon a stable and leak-free envelope. I spent significant time fitting the bright pink colored cloth to the frame, checking and recaulking the seams with a liquid rubber of my own devising. Once I'd draped the fabric on the frame, I applied some additional padding to ensure that none of the frame joints would rub the envelope. Even empty, the bright magenta silk looked splendid.

Next up was the steam engine. This was the means of propulsion and steering for the aetherigible. I will not bore you with a description since you are no doubt well familiar with the powerful engines of our times. All components checked out in working order, and I lit a quick fire to test the propellers. They began turning steadily, the engine giving off the familiar soft *chuff-chuff-chuff* sound.

All that was left to do was to insert the new gauge that I needed to monitor overall pressure. Without it, I could not set the engine to the optimum pressure when I switched it to operate in its second mode generating nyx.

To my great relief, once I'd cooled the engine, the gauge screwed on perfectly without any refitting. I double checked all of the mounts of the engine to assure nothing would come loose during flight. The tanks held enough water and the firebox had some fuel in it to test the new gauge and begin filling the envelope while I fetched more of both.

With the flip of a switch to lock down the piston for nyx generation, the engine was purring like a kitten. I checked the gauge. It rose for a time, and then the exhaust valve kicked in to maintain a steady 250 psi. I heard the hiss from the outlet pipe up in the envelope that meant nyx production had begun. I picked up the altimeter Mr. Crenshaw had given me and kissed it before I fixed it in place beside my pilot chair.

Everything seemed to be running well, so I threaded a line through the pulley mounted on the edge of the roof and threw a good length of the rope down to the ground. I climbed back into the attic and jogged downstairs and out the side door to tie up a load of firewood. In the yard, I filled two buckets with water and climbed the stairs again, trying not to slosh. As I passed the second floor, from down the hall I could hear the click of Charles' claws leaping down from the bed, but luckily I'd closed the door to the bedroom and he couldn't get out. I held still for a moment, hoping Dr. Jepson wouldn't call out to me.

Back up on the roof, the envelope was bobbing nicely above the platform. I filled the two tanks that acted as ballast. Next I grabbed the rope and pulled up the firewood then stowed it in the bin beside the boiler. With the aetherigible now supporting its own weight, I placed Papa's toolbox on board, and I untied all of the lines but one and coiled them aboard. I straightened up and pushed back my hair, adjusting the goggles on top of my head.

A certain breathlessness overtook me, but I tamped it down. I would not let giddy excitement overcome my methodic departure.

What was left to do? A name, an aetherigible must have a name. Remembering the avian name of the speedy airship I had missed that afternoon, I dipped my fingers into the port side water tank and sprinkled a few drops on the platform.

"I christen thee Kestrel."

The sun had gone down, and dark night covered the roof, though I could see the area around the aetherigible from the little glow of the fire in the furnace beneath the boiler. Down on the ground, light streamed out from the house. Emmoline must have returned and lit the gaslamps. I saw the reassuring sight of a policeman making his way along the alley swinging a lantern. They had promised to keep watch during the night. I patted my hair. I knew I should depart, but still I hesitated. What had I forgotten?

Ah, a lady never went out in the evening without a hat. A second thought popped into my head. My goodness gracious, Mr. Goff's trousers were still hanging in the bathroom!

I flung myself back inside the attic and lightly ran down the stairs, taking care to make no noise. I pinned a hat onto my hair, a small but stylish little number with a feather extending jauntily from one side. I crept down the hallway and eased the trousers off of the hook. Charles began barking. I heard Dr. Jepson calling to me, but I would not be deterred. One more trip out the attic window and I would be in pursuit of twin thieves.

As I climbed over the sill, a man's shout from the alley drew my attention for a second. A night breeze had sprung up, and I craned my neck around to the roof to discover a most distressing fact. The aetherigible had slipped its last tiedown ring and was rising! I dropped the trousers, raced up the slope of the roof, and flung myself onto the last length of rope dragging along the flat of the roof.

Pull as though I might, I could not rethread the line through the ring.

Imagine my surprise when a stronger gust of wind lifted the Kestrel up even further above the roof, and with it, clinging to the rope, me.

I could hear the policeman on the ground now shouting in earnest, though I could not make out what he said. In an instant he was joined by two of his fellows.

I do not think I flatter myself to state that in spite of the danger, I did not lose my head. I climbed the rope as quickly as I could in my skirts, and shucking all ideas of propriety, swung one leg up over the side of the platform, exposing my drawers to the astonished policemen on the ground.

Once aboard, I stood to gather myself and just then I discovered another distressing fact.

I was not alone.

From the glow of the boiler furnace chamber, I could see that on the aft end of the platform, a man sat in my place in the pilot seat, eyeing me.

"You!" I shouted.

The young thief from the market lounged back in the chair, one hand casually draped across the tiller.

"What in the blazes are you doing on my aetherigible? Get off right now!"

He leaned to look over the side.

"I'm afraid that's not possible. I beg your pardon."

I looked down and saw the roof of our house shrinking rapidly, a black pile of cloth barely discernable off to one side. "Mr. Goff's trousers," I wailed.

He looked at me in confusion.

My anger exploded. "First you steal bread and then you try to steal the Kestrel. What do you have to say for yourself?"

He met my eyes and shook his head once. "I did steal that bread, but it wasn't my intent to steal this...what did you call it?"

"Her name is the Kestrel, and she is an aetherigible," I stomped one foot in annoyance. The very idea, the likes of him questioning me.

"An ayyy—what?"

"A—thurr—ridge—ibble," I pronounced slowly.

"Oh, you mean an airship."

"Certainly not. An aetherigible." I frowned sourly at him.

"Those police down there saw me, and I didn't want to end up in jail. I was only hiding. I didn't mean to steal the whatever-you-call-it."

My pulse sped faster and my face grew hot. It is a small fault of mine, exploding over little things. I picked up a large wrench from the tool box. "Get out of that pilot's seat right now, I'm warning you."

He gripped the tiller with one hand. "But miss, you don't have a pilot. Don't you need me to fly this thing?"

My anger boiled up like water in a tea kettle. "It's *my* airship. I'm the pilot, you dunderheaded idiot!"

I rushed at him, and swung the wrench as hard as I could. He caught my arm mid-air, and the wrench flew out of my grip and over the side.

"Now look what you made me do! I might need that later." I watched the wrench spin as it fell down to the land below.

He stood up slowly from the seat still holding my arm in his grasp. I met his eyes, and his brow furrowed then relaxed again. A softness came over the corners of his eyes, and I felt an odd warmth in my stomach.

"Do I know you?" he asked.

I jerked my arm away. "I watched you steal bread in the market. But no, you don't know me."

He angled his head, searching my face with his eyes. "No, not then, I think remember you from before that."

I snorted. "I should say not." The effrontery of this young man. As though I would be acquainted with someone like him.

I took a menacing step forward, and he raised both hands to show he meant no harm. He stepped to one side of the seat then further away around the boiler toward the bow rail ten feet away, keeping his eyes on me all the while.

At this point two strong yet unrelated sensations struck me at once. I was flying! A keen excitement thrummed in my head. But at the same time, I found myself eyeing the interloper with deep suspicion, and it rather ruined the effect. I decided I'd best turn my mind to practical matters.

I checked the boiler and looked around. "We're flying too low. Any tall tree in our path will knock us from the sky." I steered the ship to a more northerly direction, then hit the switch to generate more nyx. I arranged my skirts and took my place in the pilot's seat.

He kept watching me as he inched his way over to stand by the forward rail.

"If it wouldn't be too much trouble, could you put me down now, society girl?"

A flash of anger coursed through me at that society girl comment. How ludicrous, given my situation, but what did he know?

Wanting to be rid of him, I almost descended, then an awful realization hit me.

"No. It's not possible. To descend, I would need to open the envelope and let out nearly half of the nyx. But I can't. I—I forgot to put in a valve. Besides, it would take me another two hours to make her buoyant enough to fly again. I don't have time."

"But I have somewhere to go. That is, there's somewhere I have to be."

"You should have thought of that before you stole her." I hoped he could see my scowl in the darkness.

CHAPTER 5

A JUMPING OFF POINT

My unwilling passenger slid down to sit on the floor of the platform, resting the back of his head against the rail. As we reached a higher altitude, a keener wind began to blow, ruffling his dark hair. I put on my goggles and buttoned my coat. Unlike me, he wasn't dressed for flying, and he put his arms around himself in an attempt to keep from shivering in the cool night air.

"You could sit over there, to get out of the wind." I pointed at the leeward rail.

He nodded once, and moved. I checked the altimeter, switched off the nyx, and sat back down in my seat. In spite of his interference, my heart again soared as Kestrel ascended to a higher level. I felt right, for the first time. I was flying, and the air was the environment where I belonged.

Opening the map compartment, I took out the journal and began to write.

"What are you doing?"

I didn't answer him. He could just keep wondering. I continued writing.

"You're floating high up in the sky, and you've decided to write a book?"

A shot him another glare. Now that my eyes had adjusted a bit, I could see his white teeth in the light of the waxing gibbous moon. I was astonished to see he was smiling. He was clean shaven, and his jaunty grin was wide and perfect. He had a deep dimple in one cheek, and the light wind mussed his hair.

"I'm Henry Thorne. What is your name?"

He was still looking at me, and as our eyes connected, I lost my breath and didn't answer. It must have been a gust of wind.

He smiled. "I assure you, princess, I didn't steal her. I understand that high society and good manners require an introduction, but as you can plainly see, there isn't anyone here who can introduce me to you."

Princess? My irritation at his impudence rushed back in, tamping down the exhilaration I felt over the success of my airship experiment.

"It isn't that. It's just—I'm not sure you would make a desirable acquaintance."

"Oh, yes, the bread stealing thing." The smile slid off of his face.

"And you stole this airship," I reminded him.

"But I told you. I didn't mean to take your ship. Those policemen were following me, and I was trying to dodge them by climbing up on your roof. I only meant to hide, not to leave."

"Ah, and so she untied herself?"

He fell silent.

I busied myself with adjusting the controls, then sat back and took hold of the tiller again.

"You know, I never imagined flying would be like this," he said.

"Have you never gone up in an airship?"

His eyes took on a wistful look. "I think I did once, when I was small, but I have no memory of it. Of course an affluent young lady like you probably flies all the time."

Another flurry of annoyance rose up in me, but I didn't answer him. True, I had ridden the Columbia Airship Line to Chicago three years before, accompanying my father on business. But it had only been the slow steerage variety of airship, not the fast sleek queen of the airship line, the Peregrine, so it could hardly be said I had vast experience with flying. Who did this thief think I was? Considering it, I found my one previous experience could not come close to my current exhilarating ride through the night sky.

The wind hit me, and though the month was July, I shivered. Maybe my flight jacket was not quite as warm as I'd hoped. But I wasn't about to let on to him that I was cold.

He leaned his head back against the rail and stared up at the stars. We sat for a time in uncomfortable silence, until a loud rumble emanated from my midsection. I saw his head swivel back toward me. My stomach growled again, in a most audible and unladylike way.

"Are you hungry?" He was smirking at me.

"I do beg your pardon. Unlike some people, I didn't manage to steal a meal today. You see, my father was attacked today, and I...."

I broke off speaking, because to my complete and utter surprise, unexpected tears were flowing from my eyes for the second time in one day, and I began gasping as though I could not breathe.

In an instant he dropped all the teasing. Concern showing plainly on his face, he rushed to my side. He gently removed my goggles, placed them onto the floor, and his arm slid around my shoulder as I gasped.

He helped me bend forward, murmuring softly into my ear: "It's all right, just breathe slowly. Take one breath in, then slowly out...calmly now. There we are."

Quite inappropriately for a stranger, he patted my upper back. With his warm side against mine, I calmed down and regained my composure. Stealing a sideways glance, I could see his face in the small glow from the furnace, and I thought he looked unhappy.

"Don't cry," he said.

I gulped, and attempted to recover my dignity. I said it before, I can't abide excessive emotion. It's messy and generally unproductive. I wasn't happy to have lost my composure in front of a stranger, but his kindness made it a little easier to bear, even if he was a total cad.

"Better now?"

I nodded.

"Would you like something to eat?"

I nodded again. He took his arm from around me and began fishing around in his pockets, then he pulled out something wrapped in brown paper.

"I hate to profit from your ill-gotten gains," I said, wiping my eyes, then taking it from him.

"You aren't. I bought that one fair and square this evening."

I gobbled down the ham sandwich in a most unladylike way. Perhaps you already spotted my biggest mistake in making preparations. Though the onboard storage bins stood ready, I forgot to stock food for the journey. Naturally, I had a solution in mind, but it annoyed me to realize it would result in lost time.

"I really would like to know your name," he said.

"Theo—it—it's Theodocia Hews."

He stood and bent one arm in front of him to make a little bow. "Well, Miss Hews, I am most delighted to formally make your acquaintance."

The fact that he'd given me his sandwich and his polished manners came as quite a surprise. I didn't expect such things from a common thief. He didn't seem to fit the stereotype, as he didn't seem ugly or threatening at all.

He returned to his side of the platform, and I pulled out my journal again.

"What are you writing?"

"It might be difficult for you to see the need, but since this is the first flight of my aetherigible, I am taking scientific notes on her performance. Altitude, engine pressure, steering—" I looked up at the envelope, which still appeared to be turgid with gas. "—the performance of the envelope design, and so on. I wouldn't expect you to understand."

"She's a very—er—unusual ship."

"She is my prototype."

"Of course, you might make improvements."

I raised one eyebrow at him.

"She slews in the wind."

I snorted again. He did seem to provoke the most unladylike noises from me.

"Of course she slews. I have to aim upwind in order to maintain a northwesterly course. This isn't some ballooning pleasure cruise. It's powered flight."

"If those steering fins were reshaped, I think she might make better time."

"I have neither the tools nor the parts to attempt a refit."

"I think she could go faster if you—"

I exploded. "What could you possibly know about aetherigibles? Have you built one before? Or maybe you are employed by an Airship line?"

I was being rude, interrupting him like that, it's true, but now he had my dander up.

"No, of course not, I told you I've only been on an airship that one time, it's just that—"

"Well then since you have no particular expertise, perhaps you should keep your ideas to yourself."

Henry hunkered down by the rail, turning up his collar and wrapping his arms around his knees.

He said no more, and after a time, judging by the way he'd slumped over to one side, I think he fell asleep.

I threw another piece of wood into the furnace and set my goggles back into place over my eyes. The hour was very late, or very early, depending on how you looked at it, and the Kestrel soared over the dark landscape with her quiet, rhythmic *chuff-chuff* as we steamed toward Indianapolis.

I wanted to calculate our speed, but without being able to fix landmarks on the ground below, and with no watch to time our passage from one map point to the next, that was impossible. Struggling abreast of a crosswind, the Kestrel seemed to be creeping along.

With no further interruptions from my passenger, I began to relax. According to the altimeter, we were cruising at about six hundred feet, and now that we were leaving the outskirts of Cincinnati behind, the ground below was black and featureless save for an occasional farm light. As we passed over one such point of light, I heard a dog begin barking and the sound carried through the clear air as though he were close by. It made me jump. Realizing we were high in the air and he was on the ground, I chuckled to myself, wondering what poor Rover must think of us.

None of this interrupted the slumbers of Mr. Henry Thorne.

The wind that had caused us to slew died down, and I was able to point her nose more or less directly toward my stopping point of Indianapolis, which was located to the northwest of Cincinnati, though I couldn't be sure where it was without seeing landmarks. Instead I steered by the stars. I thought to myself it certainly was a good thing I had spent a good many nights up on the roof to acquaint myself with their positions.

Hand on the tiller, I settled myself a little more comfortably in my chair, wondering if we were making more than twenty miles per hour. The moon slid behind some high, thin strips of clouds, and the air felt thin and chilly for a midsummer's night. The wind finally died down.

Exhaustion dragged at my bones, my eyes grew heavy, and then in spite of my best efforts, slumber took me.

◊◊◊◊◊◊

A bright beam of light hit my face and I awakened. The sky was glowing with crimson dawn. Henry still slept. In the slanting early morning sunbeams, I examined his face. He was handsome, devastatingly so. His nose and mouth were symmetrical, and he wore no mustache or beard, though he needed a shave.

Distracted by the sight of his face, I observed that his eyes were set off by arched brows of exactly the perfect thickness. Not so thick so as suggest a base or bestial nature, but rather just thick enough to suggest manliness and strength. He had a very attractive face, for a thief. As I gazed at him I wondered to myself—what would Julia think of him?

In the quiet of the morning I sighed and stretched my arms up over my head. The air was almost dead still, with only a hint of a breeze.

Pulling myself upright in my seat, I looked around. Across the grassy fields, spider webs lined with silvery droplets sparkled in the early rays of the sun.

And then I realized something. We were low—too low. With a start, I noticed the fire had gone out. Without propulsion, we'd drifted eastward off course and lost buoyancy.

I scrambled around the boiler to see what lay before the aetherigible. We passed over a wide creek. I saw cultivated farm fields, and not too far away, right in our path, a tall hill crowned with trees. At our current altitude, we would soon be experiencing an unplanned and dangerous stop.

"Henry!" I shouted. "Wake up and help me."

He jerked upright and looked about.

"We've lost altitude and drifted. Dump the water." I opened the door of the little furnace and scooped out the cold ashes with my hands. The light morning breeze whipped the fine powdery ash all around, and I shut my mouth tight. It was a mercy I still had my goggles on. I shoved paper and kindling inside, frantic to light the fire.

"What water?" asked Henry.

"Those ballast tanks, one on each side. There's a plug at the bottom. We have to lighten up."

He pulled the plugs and water began gurgling out. I had a tiny fire started, but the pressure was still too low.

I glanced over my shoulder. The trees loomed larger and larger.

"It's not draining fast enough," he said, his eyes wide. "We have to land. Let the gas out of the envelope."

"I can't open it, it will escape too fast and we'll crash. We have to rise. Find something and start bailing."

He hunted around in the boxes and cupboard, but found nothing, so he unlatched the tops of the tanks and began using both hands to dip water out of the tanks.

I shoved in the rest of the kindling, hoping a hot fast fire would heat the boiler enough to begin making nyx.

I flicked the gauge with my finger, but the pressure was still far too low.

Like hoary old giants standing on the crest of the hill, their arms upraised and tossing in the breeze, the trees waited to grab us.

"We aren't going up," he said.

"I see that. Start throwing things overboard."

I crammed more wood into the overstuffed furnace, and Henry began heaving the crates overboard. He broke the empty food cupboard loose and tossed it too. I picked up my pilot's chair and threw it over the rail. I threw the rest of the wood and the wood box over. Still, the Kestrel would not rise.

My eyes darted around, and I considered what was left. "Jettison the tanks."

"What?"

"They're steel, and they weigh a lot. Break them loose and throw them over."

He kicked at the starboard tank and the remainder of the water splashed everywhere. Once it broke free, he hurled it over the rail. When he did, Kestrel's platform tilted down four feet on the port side. I threw myself starboard trying to counterbalance the remaining tank. Henry kicked at it, and a section of the rail broke and took the tank with it over the side.

The platform leveled, but we'd only risen a few feet.

"What else?" yelled Henry.

I cast my eyes around, but there was nothing left but Papa's toolbox. He spotted it, and looked at me, the question on his face.

"Oh no, I can't. Not that. It's Papa's."

He bent to the firebox and adjusted the small louvers on the back and sides of the furnace.

"What are you doing?" I wanted to smack his hand away, but I held myself in check.

"I'm giving it more air to make it burn hotter," he said.

"We're not going to make it."

He opened the door and took off his coat and began fanning the fire, which glowed white with each puff. As I watched, the pressure rose higher. We were starting to generate nyx.

We were almost one hundred feet up in the air, and fifty feet away from the trees. Still too low to fly over the treetops.

I picked up the toolbox and hefted it. Henry watched me, not saying a word.

I closed my eyes and dropped it over the rail. We popped up a couple more feet, and down below, the tools hit the ground with a crash. Henry resumed fanning madly. Twenty feet from the trees...ten feet.

"It's no use," he said. "I'm the extra weight. I'll jump into the tree."

"You're crazy."

He ignored me and rubbed his hands together, eyeing the fast-approaching tree to time his jump.

"Don't!" I turned to brace myself for the impact. "Get down on the floor!"

For a moment, his eyes met mine.

He put one hand on the rail, the muscles corded in his neck, and he jumped.

CHAPTER 6

DOWN ON THE FARM

He hit a branch about one quarter of the way from the top of the tree, clung on for a second, then fell off. I would have watched him fall, but at that moment, the Kestrel hit the uppermost branch of the tree with a great crash, and I was a trifle occupied with being thrown violently sideways.

The platform jerked with the impact, and I grabbed onto the rail. The platform split under my feet, and the envelope bounced and scraped upwards. The platform caught one branch, breaking it, then it hit another, and then what was left of my poor aetherigible with me clinging to it broke free and floated on past the tree.

"Henry?"

There was no answer.

Keeping a tight grasp on the rails one hand, I reached up onto the boiler and released the pressure, then I loosened the seal where the pipe entered the envelope to let the nyx escape—the place where I should have put a valve.

The Kestrel floated drunkenly another thousand yards, then the broken platform dragged along over a field of grain for a few moments. When she finally came to a halt, I shut the louvers on the furnace to smother the fire, climbed over the rail, and ran back across the field as fast as my skirts would allow.

I skidded to a stop under the trees, looking up into the one that had caused us so much trouble. A few leaves fluttered down, but I couldn't see Henry anywhere in the branches.

"It is hard work, adventuring," his voice said.

I rushed around the tree and there he was, sitting up against the trunk holding one arm, blood dripping down his forehead and into one eye. His dark wool jacket and vest, already shabby, was torn to ribbons. I bent closer. The cut on his head was only a scratch. It didn't look too bad to me and I felt a rush of relief.

"Are you hurt?" I asked.

He gave me a cavalier look. "I've been better."

I tore a strip off of my petticoat, wiped his face, and bound up his head.

"Is your arm broken?"

He extended his left arm and bent it again. "I don't think so. Only sprained"

"That is lucky." I put my hand on his ankle. "What about your legs?"

"I have two."

"Very funny. I didn't see what happened after you slipped from the branch."

He smiled crookedly up at me. "I found another one, then another, and another. You look funny in those goggles."

Irritated, I reached up to take off my goggles and push my hair out of my face. At some point in the crash I had lost my hat, and my hair had come tumbling down.

"You are very troublesome," I said. "You know, you could have been killed. Stay here. I'll be back."

I strode away and found the toolbox lying not too far down the hill. The wooden box itself was shattered, but most of the metal tools had survived the fall. I sorted through them, looking for a small latched case which I found off to one side. I thrust it into my pocket and gathered up the tools in my arms.

Henry's voice echoed down the hill. "I would offer to help you, but..."

"Rest there. I'll have us out of here in no time," I said.

"What, in that airship? Is it still in one piece?"

Ignoring him, I sat down upon the ground and took the case from my pocket. I hoped against hope the contents had survived the fall.

Opening the lid, I was delighted to see that thanks to the shaped velvet lining, it had. I took out a delicate set of folded wings and fixed them to the little clockwork body. A pencil and strip of paper lay in the bottom of the case. I scribbled some words and then slipped the paper inside the slot in the body. Looking across the field at the river, I calculated numbers for a moment then I depressed a series of buttons, slid a lever, and wound up the clockwork with the key from the case.

The little bird fluttered up out of my hands and away across the field.

"Very pretty. Now help me up, we should get going." He struggled to get to his feet.

"Oh no, there's no need for that, you can sit a little longer. Someone will be along to get us. I sent the clockwork bird."

"You're joking."

"I never joke."

He straightened up and leaned back against the tree. "How can a mechanical bird go find help?"

"I set the controls."

He laughed. "You're pulling my leg."

"No, I'm not. It's true whether you understand it or not. That was one of my father's devices, and I am familiar with this part of Ohio. That wide creek was the Little Miami River we passed over."

He took a step and winced.

"Stop that at once." I grabbed his arm.

"I can manage well enough."

"Well, if that's the case, you go ahead. I'm going to wait here." I sat down in the shade.

"I think I see a road down there. I'll come back to get you as soon as I find someone to help us."

"Suit yourself." I smiled and waved as he limped off. While I waited, I took a moment to look around for my hat, but it had vanished, so I sat back down and tried to exercise patience.

Not twenty minutes later, a horse-drawn farm wagon appeared from across the field. Henry waved at me from his seat next to the driver.

The farmer pulled back on the reins and once the horses stopped, he climbed down.

"How do?" he said, briefly tipping his derby hat.

I ran up and gave the man a hug.

"I hardly think that's necessary," said Henry, frowning as he clambered down from the wagon. "This gentleman was more than happy to interrupt his trip to come pick us up but you don't need to throw yourself at him."

Wasn't it just like my uncle, a taciturn man at all times, not to mention who he was when Henry had flagged him down on the road? He raised one eyebrow and his eyes sparkled with his little joke as he took the flying bird out of his pocket and held it aloft.

I took the bird back from his outstretched hand. "Uncle Adolphus, I'd like to introduce Henry Thorne."

Henry's eyebrows rose high under his bandage, and I must admit, I burst out laughing at the look on his face. Clearly, he'd expected some sort of thanks from me, thinking he himself was the one who'd found someone to help with our rescue.

"Have heard any news of the Abstractionists lately, niece?" asked Uncle Adolphus in his German accent.

"Um—not lately, uncle," I lied. "They still haven't admitted you?"

He shook his head glumly. "I just sent off my forty-forth application, but still their answer is nein und abermals nein. No and no again."

I kissed him on the cheek. "It's their loss. Thank you for coming to get us."

"No trouble at all," he said, brightening up. "Where is the aetherigible?"

◊◊◊◊◊

Chickens scattered as the horses plodded into the circle drive beside the white barn, and Uncle Adolphus jumped down from the seat to roll open the big door. On the way to the farm, I'd explained to him the horrifying events of the day before. He expressed deep concern over my father's injury and the theft of the vocalizer, then he tut-tutted my predicament. I'm not sure why, but I left out the part about the near-theft of the Kestrel, nor did I share any other details about Henry.

My mother's Uncle Adolphus—he's my great uncle, but I have always called him Uncle Adolphus—was an accomplished tinkerer, and with his tools and help, I hoped to be able to refit and get back into the air. I'd woken in time to see the prevailing winds had carried me close to his farm thanks to sheer luck.

"I think I have just the thing you need, niece." He led me inside. Henry trailed along behind me.

It had been years since I'd visited, and I must confess my mouth flew open as I took in his workshop.

Instead of horse stalls, tack rooms, or grain bins, mechanical gadgets of all types met my eyes. My uncle had converted his largest barn into a marvel of modern steam equipment.

The floor was swept clean of straw, and a gleaming line of boilers and engines in varying sizes stood at attention down one entire side. Hooks covered one wall, holding tools of every shape and size. A sizeable drill press, a table saw, and a lathe and grinder stood on their own metal legs.

What caught my eye was the wide oak worktable down the center of the great barn. Whizzing gizmos, wondrous gewgaws with clattering appendages, and silvery tooled metal parts of works in process crowded each other for space.

"Uncle Adolphus! I had no idea you had moved your workshop out of the shed and into the barn."

He smiled and ducked his head modestly. "It is my little hobby."

I looked around to see Henry's reaction to these riches. He was standing transfixed next to the drill press, running his hand over the smooth, painted steel guard.

"My father had one like this," he said.

"Come over here, niece. This is what I want to show you."

Uncle Adolphus stood next to a long cloth-covered shape. He pulled the covering aside with a flourish, and there propped up on sawhorses was a beautiful japanned fourteen-foot-long open boat hull.

I gasped at the magnificence of his craftsmanship.

"Uncle, I cannot possibly take your boat. It is a work of art. And wouldn't it be too heavy for my envelope to carry?"

He put a hand on the hull. "She is exceptionally lightweight. I meant to add a top and launch her in the Ohio, but my most recent reading tells me this boat is too small and the bottom is too flat. I want to build myself a proper boat and so she is yours. May I ask what gas are you filling the envelope with?"

"Nyx. It is my own discovery." I detailed to him my method for generating the lifting gas.

He gulped. "That's hydrogen you're making! Don't you know it explodes? It is a wonder you didn't blow yourself up with the fire under the boiler!"

My stomach sank. I had a broken bamboo platform, a useless boiler, an intact envelope and frame, and no lifting gas. Papa's vocalizer seemed to be slipping beyond my reach.

"I can't use steam vapor for lifting, the condensation inside the envelope cools it too quickly."

He patted my arm. "Don't look so sad. The hydrogen can be made safer with a few simple changes to your design."

That perked me up and we quickly got to work. Even with his left arm bound up in a sling, Henry proved to be an able mechanic's assistant. How, I don't know. Maybe he had a natural knack for fixing machines. Before long, we had the revised boiler and gas generator installed aft in the new keel. Uncle Adolphus also made some modifications to the envelope framework to place it higher above the deck than before, away from the firebox. He also installed a series of small valves that would allow me to descend at a controlled rate, solving my biggest design blunder.

Henry discussed his suggestions about the shape of the steering planes, and Uncle Adolphus agreed, so they built replacements. They also improved the gearing of the propeller to allow greater speed. The beautiful hull already had ballast tanks built right in, complete with hand pumps that could empty them in a short time, which would help us rise quickly if we needed to.

We rolled the ship out into the barnyard, tied down some lines, and assembled the envelope, ready to fill her up.

I ran my hand along the shiny black finish. "She's beautiful."

Uncle Adolphus looked her over one more time and fired up the steam engine. He fingered the bottom edge of the pink envelope.

"A little bright for my taste, but I think she'll do. Come inside and have something to eat while she fills. I'd just fried some nice ham when your bird arrived."

Inside the farmhouse, we washed up and sat down at the kitchen table. Henry took the bandage off of his head and washed his face, and looked much more reputable. Uncle Adolphus' farm-raised breakfast of ham, eggs, and potatoes was tasty and I must confess, I ate far more than a ladylike portion. When we were finished, I offered to do the washing up.

"Young man, you cannot wear that ridiculous torn jacket and vest to go flying. Come upstairs and I will give you some of my son's things."

My bachelor cousin Anson and his mother Aunt Marguerite had been carried away in the same cholera epidemic that had taken my Mama. After their passing, poor Uncle Adolphus had been a lost soul. It did my heart good to see that he had new hobbies and was finally letting loose of his grief.

I heard a mumble of conversation and the scrape of drawers upstairs, and then Uncle Adolphus walked back down the stairs.

"He is dressing. Walk outside with me."

I thought he was leading me out so we could check the envelope, but instead, he stopped me on the wide porch and closed the door.

"Niece, who is this young man?"

I felt my face grow warm. I met my uncle's eyes. "He is my assistant pilot," I said.

"Good manners, and handy with a wrench, but are you sure it is proper to go flying about with this young man? There is a degree of intimacy floating together in such close quarters."

"He is fine, Uncle Adolphus," I said firmly.

Turning away to gaze at my aetherigible, I considered for a moment what my uncle was saying. While Henry wasn't the ideal assistant, he was not in every way bad. When the tree loomed up to threaten my safety, he had not hesitated to jump. He had been an exemplary gentleman on our journey once he'd turned loose his rough grip on my arm. Besides, I was used to looking after myself, I had no fear for my safety as long as a wrench or hammer lay close to hand. There was one obstacle to the plan—the social requirement that an unmarried young woman like me should retain the appearance of virtue at all times.

Was I safe with this stranger? For some reason the question bothered me, and I will admit, I had a moment of doubt. The truth was, I didn't know Henry at all. And some of what I knew about him—the incident in the market—wasn't good. And I did have my reputation to think about.

A young woman who keeps the company of men without benefit of a chaperone would never be invited to society balls. I harrumphed as I considered it. As a rule, I do not frequent balls. They are frivolous affairs, and besides, costly dresses and dancing shoes are required. Truth be told I had not been invited to a ball since I lit Mrs. Goff's elaborately coiffed hair on fire quite by accident with a cigar while attending one such soiree two years ago, but that is a story for another time. I could hardly let such a ridiculous concern bother me.

"I fully understand what you're getting at, uncle. However, this is purely a business arrangement and I believe I am quite safe with him assisting me."

"Ah, you are probably right." He took my hand in his own. "Obsessing about propriety will do neither of us any good under the circumstances."

He looked at me closely. "But are you sure your place is in the air instead of at your Papa's side?"

He was right, and I had to face up to it. I'd tried to push the vision of Papa lying unconscious in his bed out of my mind, but his pale face flashed into my mind with my uncle's question. Was I doing the right thing?

"I want to be there with him, uncle, but it's crucial that I get Papa's vocalizer back before Friday."

I told him what was at stake, and soon he was nodding agreement with my plan.

"I could go with you, niece."

"Thank you, but it's not necessary. I can do this. Besides, I don't think my airship would carry three."

Glancing over into the yard I could see the envelope filling nicely, bobbing in the air several feet above the top of the upright steam engine. We returned into the house, and Uncle insisted on giving me food suitable for travel. While I tidied up in the kitchen, he took Henry back into the barn to fill a new toolbox with Papa's tools and load some spare parts on board.

Watching out the kitchen window as I wiped the dishes dry, I saw the two of them huddled, heads together, behind the stern.

When I walked out to the barnyard, she had finally lifted and was playfully pulling at her ropes. Uncle Adolphus waved me over to her stern.

There in beautifully painted gold script letters was her name. *KESTREL TWO*.

"Oh Uncle Adolphus! How can I ever thank you enough?"

"That last bit was young Henry's idea," said my uncle, his eyes twinkling.

Henry stood straight and tall beside the steps, waiting to assist me aboard. He somehow had found time to shave, and wore a dashing two-piece black suit with a gold-toned vest over a crisp white shirt. Uncle Adolphus had fitted him with a cunning assembly of gear-jointed brass tubes mounted on a leather sleeve to allow him the use of his injured left arm. He wore Anson's top hat, since my poor departed cousin no longer had any need for it, and a shiny pair of shop goggles rested on the brim.

"Wait one moment, I must fetch two more things." Uncle Adolphus hastened into the house.

I looked over the new Kestrel. "She's incredible," I whispered.

"She certainly looks more airworthy than her predecessor," said Henry.

I bristled at his criticism. "I don't recall asking your opinion, Crewman Thorne."

"Crewman? I thought I was Assistant Pilot. Have I been reduced in rank?" The sparkle in the lout's eyes told me he was enjoying teasing me.

"You are quite impossible."

Uncle Adolphus trotted back out from the house, a carbine rifle with a polished wooden stock cradled in his arms and a box tucked under one elbow.

"Oh uncle, I don't think we'll need that."

He pressed the rifle into my hands. "One can never be too careful. I added a revolving action. It will hold six shots." He passed the box of ammunition to Henry.

Henry turned to me with an odd, calculating sort of a look on his face.

"Miss Hews, given the task at hand, it may well be that the rest of this trip will carry some risk. I know your uncle wouldn't want you to be in any danger. Perhaps it would be best if I went on alone in your place."

Once again, I felt my ire rise, and a slight roaring sound filled my ears. My gracious, this young man knew how to annoy. I strove to remember the lessons in manners dear Papa taught me to keep from sputtering a string of imprudent words.

"Mr. Thorne, as well intentioned as your offer must be, you are hardly qualified to look after my interests better than I can. You don't even know where I need to go. I remind you that you are the hired help on this trip."

"Hired." Henry rolled his eyes. "Remind me to renegotiate my terms."

"Niece, there is one more thing." Uncle Adolphus pulled a piece of paper from his pocket and unfolded it. "I think your detour to my farm might have been a stroke of luck. I thought of this when you told me what had happened."

I took the bulletin from him and read its contents aloud. "Mr. Hiram Quigley presents: The Revolutionary Racing Steam Carriage.

"Built with strict regard to the latest technological advances, the first Racer off the manufacturing line will be exhibited to the public on the Courthouse lawn, Saturday through Wednesday.

"The Racer shall depart at 2:00 o'clock p.m. sharp Wednesday to establish a new land speed record from Dayton to Chicago. Gents: the Beautiful and Exotic Salarnier Twins, Mademoiselle Angelique and Mademoiselle Fleura, of Paris, France, will perform the Can-Can and then pilot the Racer to Chicago."

I pondered the picture on the page—a sleek, streamlined, long carriage without horses. Though its looks had more in common with a locomotive than a carriage.

"Uncle? What is the Can-Can?"

Uncle Adolphus' face turned bright red, and Henry burst out laughing but then pretended to merely cough.

"A—uh—traditional French dance, I think," Uncle Adolphus said.

Henry coughed some more.

I pushed any judgmental thoughts out of my head. "Quick, I don't have a watch. What time is it now?"

Uncle Adolphus pulled out his gold pocket watch. "It is 1:30."

I felt the blood drain from my head. "What do you think our top speed could be?"

Uncle Adolphus and Henry looked at one another. "I don't know," Henry said. "Maybe thirty miles per hour?"

My uncle pressed his heavy watch into my hands. "Here. Take this, and calculate your speed. Even if you don't reach the courthouse in time, you should be able to find them on the road."

"Uncle, I can't."

"Take it. You are my only living relative. I want you to have it." He placed the watch in my front pocket. I hooked on the chain and fob. "Now you must hurry!"

My eyes felt uncomfortably hot again and I embraced him quickly.

After he'd shaken hands with my uncle, Henry stood by the Kestrel and held out his hand. I tucked the rifle under one arm, grasped hold of his fingers and climbed the step. As I passed by him I breathed in and his clean male scent—reminiscent of the good smell of shaving soap, wood and leather, and a hint of motor oil—surrounded me. Something warm and bewildering ignited in me as I met his gaze. I let go his hand. I had the oddest sensation that I should run away, but perhaps that was just me feeling the urgent need to get to Dayton.

CHAPTER 7

IN HOT PURSUIT

Stowing the step, Henry hopped aboard and untied the last line. Kestrel Two leaped straight up into the air. Her envelope still had some give, and rippled in the breeze as she continued to fill. My heart rose with her, and the sensation was so amazing I felt like singing, though I didn't. A pleasant singing voice is not one of my talents.

"Isn't it remarkable Uncle Adolphus had that bulletin? I had intended to fly straight to Chicago, but if I'd had, I would have missed them entirely."

"So you're saying it was a good thing we hit that tree?"

I laughed. "Don't remind me. Still, things did work out. And she's so much better now."

I ran my free hand along the silky smooth black-painted gunwale. The envelope was nearly full, and she was still lifting rapidly into the sky.

Henry looked up at the fluffy white clouds way up above us. "Do you mean to reach those clouds?"

"Of course not."

I checked the altimeter. We were nearly at seven hundred feet. I shut off the hydrogen generator and switched to propulsion. The Kestrel hurtled forward through the air, prompting me to give a little involuntary laugh.

"Let's see what she's got. Crewman, stoke the furnace."

Henry complied, and with his attention, the small furnace roared when he closed the door. With her new configuration, she was a willing craft, and responsive.

Making minute adjustments to the dials and controls on the boiler, I looked over the side to see where we were, and pulled out a map to plot some locations to time her. As we cruised closer towards Xenia, I spotted in the distance the town clock tower and the four white ionic-style columns of the Greene County Courthouse.

I began scanning the ground beneath us in earnest. More and more houses appeared below us as we floated past the fringes of town. The trees parted, and up ahead I saw the point where six railroad tracks converged like spokes of a wheel. We were approaching the Xenia Railway Station at the intersection of South Detroit Street and Miami Avenue. When we were directly over the Station, I checked the watch and noted the time, and then I steered the tiller to follow the tracks that led toward Dayton.

The boiler was *chuff-chuffing* with a nice, regular rhythm, propelling us along. According to the map, the Little Miami River was four miles from the Railway Station. I kept a sharp eye out for the greenish brown ribbon of water and when we crossed over, I noted the time and made my calculations.

Unable to contain a grin, I rechecked the numbers. I tipped my head back and turned my smiling face up to the sky and put my hand back on the tiller.

"Well?" said Henry.

"Well what?"

"You were checking her speed, weren't you? How fast is she going?"

"By my calculations, twenty-five miles-per-hour."

"A horse could gallop faster."

"A horse would need to follow a road. We sail as the crow flies, which is a more direct route."

"Shouldn't you give our speed in knots?"

I exhaled, trying not to be annoyed. "Did you see me tossing out a chip-log on a line like a sailor? This is an aetherigible, not an oceangoing ship. There is no water. We measure miles-per-hour."

"I only thought—"

"Well don't."

I would not let his silly questions interfere with my good mood.

I rode along in silence for a time, a keen wind in my face. Looking down over the side, I could see the smoke from the stovepipes of the farms below slanting at an angle, and the small branches of the trees were tossing in the breeze. As if he'd read my mind, Henry piped up once more.

"She's slewing again. I wonder, how fast is the wind blowing?"

I wasn't about to admit to him that I did not know. "It is a light breeze."

"It's pushing us sideways."

I eyed him. "I thought you made alterations to the design of the steering."

"I did. But it doesn't seem to be making any difference. On a sailboat—"

"I already told you, this is an aetherigible. Tend the furnace, please."

He threw another chunk of wood in, closed the door, and continued undeterred. "Yes, but on a sailboat, when you want to go upwind, you have to tack."

"I don't see how that makes any difference to us. We're in the air, not in the water."

"Maybe the air currents are just too fast and unpredictable for human reflexes to fly a ship."

His comments were beginning to annoy me in earnest.

"It is not a ship. And are you suggesting I am not capable of flying my own invention?"

"No. I went to a scientific lecture and—"

"Oh, did you sneak into that too?"

"Why are you being so disagreeable?"

I felt a vein in my temple begin to pulse. "You think I am disagreeable? You are the one who forced his way into this trip."

"You could have sent me off at your uncle's house, but here I am. Admit it, you wanted me aboard."

I clapped my mouth shut, determined not to let him bait me. I tried to remember why I hadn't left him behind.

After an uncomfortable silence had passed, he put another piece of wood on the fire and checked the gauges.

"I wasn't trying to start an argument. I want to help," he said in a soothing voice. "It's only that I've spent some time on boats on the Ohio talking to the river men, and the way the wind is pushing on your envelope reminds me of the sailboats trying to sail up the Ohio River when the wind is from the east."

I was reluctant to hear what he had to say. But Papa says a lady must not be prideful, so in the interest of scientific discovery, I tried to listen.

"Go on," I said.

"You would think that with both the river current and the east wind pushing on the poor little boats, they would just tie up snug somewhere and wait until the breeze comes around to a more favorable direction, but they don't. Here, let me show you."

He came to the back of the hull to crouch beside me. Taking up a piece of paper and a pencil, he began to sketch.

"This is the river. The wind is going this way, the same as the river current. The easiest way to sail is with the wind behind you."

He drew a little boat with a full sail heading downriver to demonstrate.

"I hardly see—"

He held up one finger to stop me.

"But the sailors do manage to go the other way too. This arrow is the wind. They angle their sail and zigzag their way up the wind." With the pen, he drew a back and forth line indicating what direction the boat should take.

I thought for a moment, rubbing my eyebrow with my thumb.

"We don't have a sail."

"No," he said. "But the envelope is big enough that the wind is pushing on it just like a sail. The angle that you are using now is forcing the wind straight into her. My idea is, if we turn her to one side and then the other, she'll get a little push from the wind and go faster."

"But it would be a longer distance."

"True, but the faster speed should more than make up for it. What do you think?"

I puzzled over his drawing for a moment, then looked at my watch. The time was 1:45. We still had some 12 miles to go, but at our current rate of speed, we wouldn't arrive until well after 2:00. With a pang, I realized our quarry might well be slipping away.

I looked at Henry. He was crouching very close, his arm touching mine, and even with the wind, I thought I could detect his warm scent again.

"There may be some truth in your argument."

"We aren't going to get there on time, are we? Why not give it a try?" He tilted his head.

He'd argued his side with considerable skill, and I felt my resolve weakening. I had to find the twins to find the vocalizer.

Henry could see I was wavering.

"Let me take the tiller," he said.

"You presume too much. Just tell me where to steer."

"That way." He pointed in a west-south-westerly direction.

I turned the tiller and began tacking to port. As we came directly upwind then further left, the slight buffeting we'd been feeling nearly stopped. We were now pointing in a direction that would take us left of Dayton.

"How long do we keep this heading?"

"A couple of minutes more."

"It feels wrong."

"Just give it a chance."

The farms below grew closer to one another with fewer and fewer trees between them as we came nearer to the town. The railroad tracks had slipped almost out of sight to our right.

"Now come about that way," he said, pointing to the right.

"That's starboard."

"I thought we weren't making any ocean references," he said, smiling at me.

I rolled my eyes and began heading back toward the railroad tracks.

As we continued on into the wind then to the northwest, I could see a stone quarry pass below us, its rock walls stripped bare. The Kestrel Two was slewing as badly as her predecessor. The wind was not steady, it came in gusts and puffs that gently bumped us sideways, and then let us go.

"I'm not sure this is helping." I fixed the tiller in place and pulled out my pocket watch. My stomach sank. "It's already five minutes past two. We're going to miss them."

"Maybe they'll be late in leaving."

"To set a speed record? I hardly think so."

We passed over the railroad tracks again, and I turned her nose into the wind. Up ahead, I could see the cluster of larger buildings that was Dayton.

"You're not going to tack?" asked Henry.

"No. This seems easiest. I'll point her toward the courthouse when I see it."

"What will you do when we get there?"

"I had thought I would set down, but if they've already gone..." I trailed off, uncertain. "We'll just have to see."

More and more gravel roads appeared now that we were closer. Clapboard and brick houses lined the streets behind gracious lawns.

It reminded me of Cincinnati, but with much lower hills. The summer day had grown very warm, and now and then the pungent odor of garbage drifted up.

"I'm going to start taking her lower," I said.

I released one of the valves Uncle Adolphus had installed on the envelope, and the hydrogen began hissing out. In no time we had descended to two hundred feet, to where the wind was weaker. The railroad tracks had taken a turn towards the left and now followed along beside the Mad River.

The streets were even more numerous now, and looking at the map, I thought the numbered streets had begun. I stowed the map and papers away, brought us down to one hundred fifty feet, and leveled out.

"See the two rivers meeting there? We're getting close." My heart beat faster and I peered down into the streets. We were so close to the ground now that every now and then, people walking looked up and pointed. I saw horses pulling carriages. All moving away from the city center.

"What does this courthouse look like anyway?" asked Henry.

"Uncle Adolphus said to look for a white limestone building with thick columns, like a Greek temple. He said we couldn't miss it."

"There!" Henry pointed.

And there the courthouse was, at the corner of Third and Main, just as my uncle had described. I slowed the propeller and we floated slowly toward the intersection.

The business traffic of an ordinary day—wagons and light carriages—traveled up and down Main.

As we floated closer, I saw that the lawns and streets around the impressive courthouse building were strewn with bits of paper and cast off garbage. Two men with brooms were sweeping up. A temporary grandstand had been put up, but it now sat empty save for two little boys climbing and playing along the seats. One of them spotted us and they stopped what they were doing. They both looked up in amazement, their hands shielding their eyes from the sun.

The time was now twenty past two. The Revolutionary Racing Steam Carriage was gone.

CHAPTER 8

BIRDS OF A FEATHER

Frustration washed over me. I had failed. I knew when we lifted off that we most likely would be too late, but still it gnawed at me and Henry hadn't even said he was sorry. I kicked the wood box twice, hard, and my eyes began to burn with real tears of anger mixed with pain, so I tore off my goggles and plunked down into my chair, cutting the power to the propeller to its lowest level and setting the tiller so the Kestrel would circle.

Henry cleared his throat and approached the stern. "I'm sorry. It's my fault we're late. I never should have tried tacking."

I didn't answer.

"We can catch up with them. With a boiler as large as the one in the picture, they'll have to keep stopping for coal and water. Besides, without a light, they can't drive in the dark. Can they?" He placed a hand upon my shoulder.

"But I don't know which road they're taking to Chicago."

"Maybe I can find out." He leaned way over the side and waved to the boys, who eagerly waved back.

"Hello! Can you hear me?"

"Yes sir," answered the larger of the two.

"Did either of you see the Racing Carriage here in the past hour?"

"Yes sir," repeated the larger one enthusiastically.

"We came to see the pretty ladies who kicked up their skirts!" squeaked the smaller one.

The larger boy punched him. Whether for answering out of turn, or for revealing to strangers their true purpose in attending the spectacle, I didn't know.

"Can you tell me which way the ladies went?"

The larger boy cocked his head to one side. "For a nickel I can," he said.

"Why that little—" said Henry to me.

"Shush," I said. "Do you have a penny?"

Henry dug a coin out of his pocket.

"I'll pay you a penny," I called down to the boy.

"To Chicago," said the larger one. He kept his hand on his fellow this time.

"We knew that already from the bulletin. Was there any talk about the route of their trip?"

"What street did they take out of town?" asked Henry.

At this, the two boys put their heads together and conferred. There seemed to be some disagreement about the answer, and after a moment, the smaller one pushed the larger, then the larger one took a swing, and then they both fell down on the ground fighting.

What was it with boys and their fights? I'd witnessed the neighborhood boys in Mount Belvedere come to blows over far less provocation than who would get the penny to tell us the current whereabouts of two French hussies.

Henry was looking on helplessly at this point and I was contemplating whether a blast from the carbine into the dust near the two struggling rascals would bring them into more rapid agreement when another voice spoke up.

"Sir?"

Henry crossed from port to starboard and hung his head out over that side. "Yes?"

One of the men who had been sweeping up the other side of the square had spoken. They now stood gawping up at us, their work forgotten.

"Were you asking about the dancers?" the man yelled.

"Yes, I was," answered Henry.

"It was a devil of a thing! Begging your pardon, miss."

I waved him off to let him know I hadn't taken offense. As a rule, I am not concerned about strong language, though Papa says a lady never curses.

"Can you tell me which way they were headed?" shouted Henry.

"They were headed north to get onto the National Road toward Indianapolis."

"Thank you. What time did they leave?"

"I think it might have been two o'clock, sir, though I kind of lost track of the time."

Henry nodded. "Yes, I can see how that could happen. Thank you."

I dropped the penny in payment. The man waved, picked it up once it hit the ground, and walked over to pull the rascals apart and send them on their way.

"There, you see?" Henry said to me, smiling so broadly his cheeks pushed up his goggles, "It's not over yet. We can catch them on the road to Indianapolis."

"Fire up the boiler. We're wasting time!" I put my own goggles back over my eyes.

In no time at all we were headed north up Main and across the Great Miami River.

We were still flying low and our passage had the unfortunate effect of startling not one but two teams of horses into running away. I'm ashamed to admit it, but I didn't much care, as we were once again in hot pursuit.

"I should have known they'd take the National Road. It's newly paved, after all," I said.

"They'll stop at Richmond for fuel," said Henry.

I tilted my head. "How can you possibly know that?"

"They said—the boiler is big—from that picture, it looked..." he trailed off and blinked a couple of times. "What I mean to say is it would make sense if they stopped there. For fuel." He shifted his weight from one foot to the other.

"Lucky for us, the wind has let up. Here, take this map and calculate how many miles from our current position to the next town. It should be Vandalia." I made note of the time.

Henry took the map but hesitated.

"You do know your numbers, don't you?"

"Yes of course, but...."

"Can you read a map, then?"

"I—yes. I can."

"Well then, get to it. I shouldn't have to do everything."

He went forward and spread the map out on a box, pinning it down with one arm. He bent his face close to study it, pencil in hand. I could tell he was working hard, because his tongue protruded a little bit from the corner of his mouth, though he drew it back in when he saw that I was watching.

The road below went up and down the rolling hills north of Dayton. Soon there were woods all around, with a few farms sprinkled in.

"Shouldn't we fly a little higher?" he asked.

"I don't want to lose sight of the road and miss them. You just worry about that map. I think this heavier new hull has slowed her, so I want to make a fresh speed calculation."

I tended the boiler. I drew out a funnel Uncle Adolphus had given us, and I set about adding a bit of water to make sure the tank was topped off. Then I began meticulously checking the various valves and oiling the exposed gears.

I had just begun greasing the drive shaft when a terrible cooing and squawking sound met my ears. The clamor was just the way you'd expect a large flock of birds to sound if they'd discovered some great steaming devil in their midst. But there was no devil. It was us.

A colossal airborne river of passenger pigeons lay ahead, so many that they darkened the sky. The first birds to encounter the Kestrel at the edge of their flock sensibly veered off in all directions. But as we encountered the next wave, their natural tendency to fly in tight formation got the better of them, and we sped right into their midst.

Startled birds began bouncing off of the envelope left and right. My place in the stern behind the tall boiler offered me some protection as I cowered there, but up front in the open bow, poor Henry was overrun. Or, should I say, overflown.

With the first impact he began wind-milling his arms and shouting in a fruitless attempt to fend off the birds.

"Good Gravy!" he cried.

He swung his right fist at three passing birds to no effect. As the throng of birds grew thicker, he flailed both arms around his head. Three frightened passenger pigeons veered straight into his chest and crashed to the floor where they flapped weakly around his feet.

"What in blazes? I—hey!"

Another swarm pelted him, one unfortunate bird breaking its neck on his metal-wrapped arm.

Henry snatched up the small shovel meant for the furnace ashes and began swinging. This only served to panic the birds further, and they ran into each other, flapping and scratching in their attempt to escape our headlong flight through their midst.

"Fight fair, you sorry creatures! Oof!"

Two at once bounced off of his stomach then another crashed smack into his goggles. He swung the shovel with a vengeance.

I couldn't help myself. I laughed at him.

"By Satan's fire!" he cried.

He caught one a glancing blow, then knocked down two others with one mighty swipe. Birds kept bouncing off of the envelope and flying away. The air was still thick with the sheer mass of bodies.

"I think we're losing hydrogen," I shouted, and I hit the switch to rise up, but the Kestrel did not respond.

I was beginning to think the blasted flock meant to knock us from the sky through sheer, bird-brained stupidity, then the bird encounter ended as quickly as it had begun.

The rest of the flock veered away in a cacophony of sound. Feathers spun through the air all around. More feathers stuck to Henry's black coat here and there, along with a liberal application of bird droppings. He had lost his top hat and it lay dented in the bottom of the ship. His hair stuck up every which way. A sheen of sweat covered his cheeks and forehead. I put one hand over my mouth for fear I might laugh again.

He pulled off his white-smeared goggles and spat a feather out of his mouth.

"You know, everyone always talks about how marvelous it would be to be a bird," he stated, holding himself upright with great dignity, "but I'm just not seeing it."

I tried my best, but I could not hold it in. I dissolved into helpless laughter. When my outburst subsided enough for me to gasp for breath and take another look at him, he had a rueful smile on his face and a twinkle of mischief in his eye, which of course set me off again.

"You're not hurt, are you?" he asked.

"No, I hid behind the boiler."

He looked down at the carnage around his feet. Twenty-two pigeons lay dead or maimed in the bottom of the hull. I began picking them up and dropping them overboard.

"Wait. Don't do that."

I froze, a dead bird in each hand. "Why in the world not?"

"They're good eating."

"Who eats pigeons?" I began laughing again, but Henry didn't join in this time. Instead he looked down at his feet.

"Oh my, I didn't mean to insult you...." I trailed off.

He brushed some feathers off of his coat. "It must be nice to have wealth on your side."

My face flushed hot. "You are mistaken."

"How could I be mistaken? I think having loads of money would be very nice."

I shook my head. "That isn't what I meant. I haven't explained to you why I have to find Papa's vocalizer."

Haltingly, I told him about the reduced circumstances Papa and I found ourselves in over the past few years.

"And so," I said, "if Papa doesn't deliver the finished vocalizer by Friday, the contract will be cancelled, and we'll lose our home."

His eyes softened as he listened to me.

"I didn't know that. You know, there's no shame in being poor."

He took a step toward me, and my heartbeat quickened. Uncertain of his intent, I looked down and picked a feather off of my jacket then brushed myself off briskly.

He stopped, though it seemed to me he didn't want to.

I cleared my throat. "Hopefully it won't come to that. Do you think it's possible a beak punctured the envelope? I turned on the hydrogen generator, but we aren't rising. I would like to bring this journey to a speedy conclusion, if at all possible."

"Let me take a look."

He took hold of the frame and gingerly stepped up onto the gunwale.

I felt a flutter of fear for him in my stomach. "Oh, please be careful. I didn't mean for you to climb up there."

Keeping his hands on the frame and tethers, he worked his way around, checking for holes.

"I'm not seeing anything wrong with it. This silk is surprisingly strong. Did you check the altimeter?"

I flicked the glass faceplate with my finger, and the needle began to move. "I think it was just stuck. Perhaps a bird hit it."

He climbed back down into the hull, and I let my breath out. I checked over the controls in what I hoped was a business-like manner. "I wonder, how far did we come?"

Henry shrugged.

And then I gasped. "The map, where is it...?"

He groped around in the pile of dead birds and loose feathers, then straightened back up, the dismay in his eyes mirroring mine.

"Gone."

My heart leaped into my throat and I rushed to look over the side.

"Henry, where is the road?"

CHAPTER 9

DINNER AND DRAMA

I scrambled from one side of the hull to the other, shading my eyes from the sun, but I could see no trace of the road we'd taken north out of Dayton. There were farms and woods and a narrow meandering country lane, but no Main Street. My heartbeat pounded in my head.

"Which way could it be?" My voice sounded frantic even to my own ears.

Henry peered around. "We couldn't have gone that far out of our way. How much time passed since you last checked?"

"I think we've been flying for about thirty minutes. But I hadn't set the tiller before we ran into the flock, so I think we've drifted. There's no telling where we are."

Henry scratched his chin.

"I had just figured out that Vandalia was about 18 miles from Dayton when those wretched pigeons hit me. How fast were we going?"

"I don't know, I can't guess without reaching a second landmark. And besides, I switched off the propeller because I thought we were losing altitude. This is hopeless."

"No, it's not. The National Road runs east to west, right?"

I nodded.

"And we don't know whether we've crossed it or not. We could be east or west of Main. So why don't we just head west for another half hour to be certain we're west of that road, and then go south fifteen minutes to try to cross the National Road? If we don't find it that way, we could then head north until we locate it."

"Do you think that will work?"

"I don't see why not. It's logic."

"Another oratory you sneaked into?"

"Something like that." Henry smiled.

I turned the tiller and headed west as best I could. "You know, I'm going to need a lot more than new maps to navigate properly. I'll need charts of the sun's path by date, and maybe an astrolabe to fly at night."

He laughed.

"I wasn't being funny, I mean it."

"Surely you can see the humor," he kept smiling. "It's not like we can just pick up an astrolabe along the way."

"I find very little in your comment to amuse me."

We fell into an uncomfortable silence. I couldn't decide if he was disagreeable all the time, or if he was doing it especially for me. His personality was certainly outside of my experience. I don't know whether his upbringing as a thief caused his comments to rankle so much or something else. I checked over the boiler.

"Put a little more wood into the furnace please, we've lost pressure."

"Aye aye, captain." He smiled and stepped over to the wood box.

I fixed him with a stern look. "Why do you do that?"

"Do what?"

"Tease me so dreadfully."

Henry looked somewhat crestfallen. "I didn't mean to tease. I only meant to be funny."

The silence returned, this time as thick as porridge. He tended the furnace, I greased the propeller shaft, and I stewed over whether it would be worth the loss of time to land somewhere and be done with him.

I sat in the pilot's chair gazing out over the side, trying to spot the road in the trees below. I couldn't see him on the other side of the boiler, and he was quiet in the front, save for some tuneless whistling. A worse unintended passenger I could not imagine. I decided that I'd have to ignore him.

The whistling changed to humming. From time to time, a sprinkling of feathers would fly past the boiler. Was he tidying the floor of the hull?

There was more humming, reminding me of nothing so much as a hive of happy, musical bees. Whatever his song was, it seemed to be reaching a crescendo. On the other side of the boiler I heard the metal clunk of the furnace door again, though looking at the gauge, there was no need for wood yet.

Watching the farms pass below, I began to imagine rising up through the still summer air the savory odor of some farmwife's supper cooking. A vision of pan-roasted chicken came into my mind, and my mouth began to water. Supper time was a while off yet, but I considered going aft to dig through the supplies Uncle Adolphus had loaded on board to try to find something to eat.

When I remembered my unpleasant passenger and my intention to ignore him, I pushed my hunger away. I wouldn't look. I wasn't about to let Henry win.

There were more feathers, and more metallic sounds, and the tantalizing smell grew. When a wing sailed back and hit me square in the face, I must admit, my curiosity got the better of me, and in spite of myself, I peeked around the boiler.

Henry sat on the floor of the ship. Jacket off, sleeves rolled up, and a pigeon in hand, he was plucking and humming a happy song. He looked up with an expression on his face reminiscent of a small child who has unexpectedly been given a new toy.

"Oh. Didn't see you there," he said. "Getting hungry for dinner?"

"What on earth are you doing?"

"Your uncle—the kind man—gave us a small fry pan. The first batch will be ready in just a minute." He opened the door to the firebox, poked at something inside with a long fork, and closed it again. "By the way, isn't it time to turn south?"

I closed my mouth, which was half hanging open—whether from astonishment or hunger, I don't know—and tried to arrange my face into more serious, commanding lines.

"It smells good, but don't you think we ought to be looking for the road? Two sets of eyes would—"

He held up a hand to interrupt me. "Don't worry. It runs straight as an arrow and the gray stone macadam should show up like a beacon from up here. We can't miss it...if you turn south."

Speechless, I went aft to change course and resumed my lookout over the side. Henry was now whistling a merry tune. The unmistakable clatter of china and cutlery met my ears as the delicious aroma of roast squab filled the air. My anger flared up again because he was being so thoughtful and reasonable.

"All ready for you now."

Try though I might, I found myself irresistibly pulled around the boiler again. Henry had turned a crate over, covered it with a white cloth and set two places. Two other boxes substituted for chairs.

"Henry, I appreciate the gesture, but I have to keep watch for the road."

Cast iron skillet in hand, he peered over the side. "Imagine the luck. There the road is right now!"

I rushed to his side, and sure enough, I could see a wide, straight line cutting through the trees.

"If you would turn her west and set the tiller, I think we can sit down for dinner."

I did as he said and when I returned to perch on a box, he'd served the squab, brown and succulent.

"I fried up some onions with it. I hope you don't mind."

I was confounded. How could he be so insufferably rude one moment, then turn around and be so kind and cheerful the next? I had to conclude that I did not like him one bit, though he did know how to cook a tasty pigeon.

After a time, Henry dabbed his lips with a napkin.

"I want to apologize for before. You see, I am not used to the company of ladies like you."

"No doubt that is a consequence of your chosen profession."

He looked down at his plate, consternation clear on his face. "I didn't mean to be a—"

"No?" I interrupted. "How does one accidentally become a thief?"

He didn't answer.

Looking at his arm holding his plate, I could see scars that looked like letters.

"What's that on your arm?"

He touched the place with the fingers of his other hand. "This?"

I nodded.

He dropped his eyes and began speaking softly.

"When I was nine, the cholera took my mother, two of my sisters and my baby brother. Five weeks later, my father and my other sister died too. After a couple of years, I felt like I was forgetting them, so I scratched these letters so they would be with me always."

He traced the marks with his fingertip.

"I for Isaac, K for Katherine—my parents. And Amanda, Evelyn, Rose, and Johnny. I think about them every day."

He traced the letters again, lost in his thoughts, and I could tell he'd done it many, many times before. My heart softened a little and I leaned forward to rest my hand on his arm for a moment.

"My mother died from cholera too. Where did you go then?"

"Then?" He drew his eyes back to me as though he'd been in a place far, far away.

"After they passed away."

"Oh, I went to live with my grandmother."

"Good of her to take you in."

"She's very kind. I get my sense of humor from her. My father had been supporting her before he died, since she didn't want to leave her small house down near the river. After I came to stay with her, she did the best she could to keep food on the table."

He prodded at the bones on his plate with his finger.

"She's an unusual woman, my granny. She grew up down in Kentucky and knows how to find the food the land offers. She taught me how to catch pigeons without a gun."

He paused to lick his fingers. "She used to take me with her every Sunday to set a line for catfish in the river. She'd tie on a chicken neck and a lead weight next to the big hook, and cast it in as far as she could throw. Then she'd sit down in the shade to drink elderflower wine while she waited."

A quiet little smile crossed his face, then he went on.

"She knew where to dig for chicory and cattail roots, and she'd boil curly dock and sorrel. We'd pick wild blackberries in the summer and in the fall we'd gather hickory nuts and black walnuts. She kept a flock of scrawny chickens in the yard, but she always got upset when they'd get into her garden to peck her vegetables or when they'd wander away. We had a rooster with a particularly horrible crow. 'Henry,' she'd say, 'go chase that rooster off. It sounds like he's smothering a parrot.' They were an odd flock. They were always flying up to roost in the lower branches of a tree in the yard instead of going into the coop at night like they should." His blue eyes twinkled at the memory.

"Why, it sounds like a marvelous childhood," I said.

The ghost of an expression crossed his face and he dropped his eyes to his lap before he began again.

"I helped out as much as I could, but I was small and it was hard to find odd jobs. When the river froze solid in the winter of 1874, we had to eat the chickens and the rooster. That was the year she taught me how to sneak into people's henhouses to take the eggs without disturbing the chickens. When I couldn't find any eggs, sometimes I had to take a chicken. Things were better once summer came and we could find food again. But then she got sick, and I had to find other ways to support us."

He put down his plate. "What was your mother like?" he asked.

The question took me completely off guard.

"I can barely remember her. I was very small when she died." I gazed off into the distant trees below. "She had lovely soft hair, I think the color was light brown. Sometimes I get a vision of her dressed all in white lying in bed with dim candlelight shining on one side of her face. I think it was when she lay dying. But I try not to think of that."

I put the squab leg I'd been nibbling back down onto my plate. My appetite had fled.

"I'm sorry, I didn't mean to make you remember sad things," Henry said.

I straightened my shoulders. I pride myself on my good posture. Papa always says you could use my back for a ruler it's so straight.

"No," I said. "It's not all sad. I remember she always wore a wonderful lilac scent. To this day I cannot smell the lilacs blooming in the spring without being swept back to that time in my life when my mother held me in her arms. It's a nice memory."

He sat there across from me, looking at me steadily and giving me time to go on if I wanted to.

"I would think that—" I broke off, not sure if I should say what I was thinking.

"What?"

"Doesn't your grandmother hate it that you steal things?"

He let out a short bark of a laugh.

"I told you, she was the one who showed me how to steal eggs. If my granny saw me in these clothes, she'd tell me I looked jumped up and 'afternoonified.'"

A wry smile played about his lips.

"Well, surely your parents would have preferred that you not do it?"

The corners of his mouth drew down. "Granny is sick. I took that bread so I could give her something to eat. In the past, I tried to find real work, but the only thing I could find was at the Crematory near downtown when another cholera epidemic started. After what had happened to my family, I just couldn't face that terrible place."

I stared off into the distance, thinking for a moment about what he'd just told me. We weren't so different, the two of us. We'd both suffered sorrow. And were my little nighttime excursions to find the supplies I needed for my work so different? It occurred to me he and his grandmother had only done what they'd needed to do.

"I'm ashamed to admit it, but I've taken other things, besides bread." Henry dropped his eyes to his lap. "I've fallen in with a bad crowd."

I felt a little stab of worry. "Who?"

"The Riverfront Ruffians."

I gasped. The Ruffians were a gang of young brutes who were the terror of downtown Cincinnati, and I was horrified to know that he was a part of them. This changed everything.

"You shouldn't throw in with such bad men. Couldn't you find a regular job?"

"I had no real experience, no contacts, and there's been a flood of German immigrants moving into the city. The few positions available go to the employer's friends or families."

"You should have fled the city to become a farm laborer."

"I couldn't leave Granny, she is all the family I have. If she died, I'd be all alone in the world."

That made me think of Papa lying unconscious in his bed at home. I swallowed thickly.

"I made the mistake of borrowing money from one of the Ruffians. I've been trying to pay them back, but they keep insisting I do 'little jobs' for them. Try as I might, with the cost of Granny's medicine, I can't get ahead."

"Little jobs. You mean stealing." I looked down my nose at him in disgust.

"I'm not proud of it."

I'd been wondering before what Julia might think of Henry. There was no way I could introduce them now. And my father would positively lose his mind with worry if he knew who I had with me. I began to wonder if Henry had made up that whole story about his family dying just to soften my opinion of him. I couldn't believe what I was hearing. I simply couldn't understand the flimsy reasons he'd given. Everyone has choices.

"But Henry, the Ruffians? They're just this side of murderers. Why don't you just quit? Go live someplace else far away from them?"

"I can't afford to move Granny."

"It all sounds quite hopeless," I said callously. "Maybe I should land the airship right now. I have my reputation to consider."

"You have to believe me. I come from a good family. My father never owed a penny he could not pay. This is not what I was raised to be."

I crossed my arms and glared at him.

Henry frowned. "We have come this far, and I mean to show you I am a good man. I can make myself useful." He stood up and gripped the rail, looking for a moment down at the ground below then turned back toward me. "I know I tease you more than I should. But you can't put me down on the ground and strand me here."

I fumed. Who was he to say I should not put him down? My uncle had been right. He was entirely unsuitable as a companion, and might even be dangerous. Even if he did have a sick grandmother, that was no excuse for his behavior. He'd been trying to curry my favor with the meal. What the devil had I seen in him?

I stormed aft and pulled the seals on all three envelope valves to send hydrogen hissing up into the air. The Kestrel dropped, and we floated down—closer and closer—the road now directly beneath us.

"Theo...," he said.

I would not meet his eyes.

"Theo...."

I crossed my arms and turned my back on him.

"Theodocia Hews!"

I spun around, gathering a mouthful of blistering words to fling at him, but I never got them out.

Henry stood leaning over the forward rail, pointing. "Up ahead! It's the racing carriage!"

CHAPTER 10

DOUBLE TROUBLE

There was the racer in the distance, climbing the long hill towards the state line, smoke pouring from its massive stack.

My resolve to be rid of Henry weakened. After all, he was right, he was useful. He hadn't done anything untoward so far, and maybe I'd been wrong to judge him so quickly in the midst of my anger. Our quarry was in sight, and I desperately wanted to get the vocalizer back.

"You can stay for now. Throw more fuel on the fire."

My hands trembling with excitement, I endeavored to stop the outflow of gas. He stoked the firebox until it roared and when I hit the switch, the Kestrel sprang forward like an arrow.

We flew along at a tremendous rate of speed in spite of the fact that the wind had picked up. But unlike earlier, this wind was out of the west. I began to think what worked best for speed in these conditions was to fly straight into the wind, because that way, the narrowest profile of the Kestrel was exposed—just the front. Without the wind buffeting the side of the envelope, the ride was much smoother too, with only an occasional lift or stomach-dropping fall as a gust seized us.

The keen wind whistled in my ears and we covered ground quickly, but try though we might, the racer had the advantage of greater speed and we fell further and further behind, until we could see them no more. We weren't fast enough, and I despaired again. No matter what we did, it seemed our effort would be altogether unsuccessful.

A sizeable village appeared up ahead.

"That must be Richmond, Indiana. I've never been so far out of Ohio before. They will have stopped there for fuel and water," said Henry.

We approached the village at speed. I craned my head over the side, looking up and down the dusty streets, but I couldn't see the racer.

"Where are they?"

Henry leaned over the front rail, "There!"

The racer stood idling in front of a grocer's shop, a small plume of smoke marking its location. A crowd of onlookers had gathered around. Everyone was so mesmerized at the spectacle that no one noticed us in the sky. As we drew closer, I could see a burly merchant shoveling coal from a horse-drawn wagon into the tender. An evil-looking, squint-eyed fellow stood on a ladder, carefully pouring bucketfuls of water into the tank.

"That must be their engineer," Henry said in a low voice. "Aren't you going to land?"

I shook my head. "I might hit those people. Let's look for a better spot nearby."

We veered right and soon enough, behind the row of businesses I spotted a grassy, fenced field next to a barn.

I must admit, I was feeling some trepidation, as this was our first intentional landing. We were already low and the ground rose up with a rapidity that made me hold my breath. Even with the gusty wind, we should be able to alight perfectly in the center of the field.

"Brace yourself," I said clutching the tiller just before impact.

We hit with a bump, then the wind tipped the hull up and dragged us sideways across the grass toward the fence. We hit something solid and lurched to a sudden stop.

Henry leaped out and knotted some lines around the fence posts to secure the Kestrel. Shaking a bit, I climbed over the side and walked around to the other side of the hull. Henry stood by the fence, hands on his hips, looking at a cow lying flat on its side on the ground.

"Now that was hardly sporting," he said.

"Oh dear, I didn't notice her. I was too busy steering. How is she?"

"I think she's dead."

"The poor thing. Don't get any ideas of cooking beef in the firebox. We must hurry."

"I don't know," he said, "maybe we should stop to come up with a plan first."

"A plan? Who ever heard of such nonsense? I mean to demand my property from them in front of that crowd."

"But they—"

"But nothing. Come on!"

I took off toward the grocer's, Henry following some distance behind me.

"Henry, keep up."

I darted down the alley and cut between two buildings to emerge amidst the crowd. The people cheered loudly until a billowing haze of smoke rolled through and caused them to dart this way and that to escape. I fought my way through to the front, but the racer was already pulling away. Through the choking cloud I could just make out two blonde heads in the cockpit wearing tiny, ridiculous red hats and gleaming copper goggles. The engineer stood in back, shoveling coal into the firebox as fast as he could.

Henry made his way through the people. He found me shaking my fist after them and releasing some unladylike words I'd heard once at the Cincinnati rail yard that I'd saved for just such an occasion.

"Don't—"

I rounded on him angrily. "Don't what? Why were you lagging so far behind? You've caused me to miss them."

"It's all right. They'll stop again for fuel in Knightstown."

I looked at him, not understanding.

"Knightstown? How in the world could you possibly know that?"

His eyes darted around and he coughed.

"It makes sense they would stop there, it's halfway between Richmond and Indy."

"Indy? Do you mean Indianapolis? I thought you said you'd never been outside of Ohio before. How can you know that?"

He dashed one hand across his forehead. "I am, er, a keen student of geography."

"You are a thief and a liar. You must have heard someone here say that."

"So only the privileged class can have knowledge of geography? What do you want to do now, duchess? Since rushing in hasn't worked?" He smiled at me rakishly.

He did know how to irritate me.

"Stop wasting time. We need to get back to the aetherigible before the owner of that cow heads home."

We left the crowd and scurried back up the alley. Henry untied all the ropes but one and I scrambled over the gunwale, flashing my petticoats without meaning to. I caught him looking at me, a rapt expression on his face, which exasperated me further as I yanked my skirts down. How I wished I had Mr. Goff's trousers at that moment.

I scowled at him. "Stop gawking and cast off."

We took to the sky and once again, we could see them steaming along on the road ahead of us, but try as we might, we could not catch up.

We sailed along without incident, but not being able to see them made me anxious.

Henry kept the boiler stoked.

"Don't worry," he said. "I have a plan. If we go straight to Indianapolis, we should get well ahead of them when they stop in Knightstown."

"But how will we know when or where to put down to try to catch them?"

"Once we're ahead, anywhere on the road inside the city will do."

Time stretched on. I sat in my seat tapping my foot.

Henry made another foray into conversation.

"You know, if you are tired of steering, I could take a turn to let you rest."

"You wouldn't know how," I said coldly.

"Well, I have held the string of a kite, how much harder could it be?"

This was such an affront that I made no answer.

He tried to make other small talk, but I wasn't in the mood. Truth be told, I didn't think much of his plan, but I didn't have one of my own. It seemed like everything about him grated. Finally, after a long period of silence, I could hold myself in no more.

"Something has been bothering me. If you are so worried about your grandmother, why didn't you even mention it until today?"

"I think about her every moment."

"Then why aren't you at home taking care of her in her sickbed? You can't have thought of her much if you left her all alone."

"I didn't say she was—you see, they—blast it, you do have a way of twisting a man's words."

He turned and sat down, his back to me in the front of the hull.

The silence stretched between us for over two hours more, until the sun dropped lower into the clouds and we reached the outskirts of the thriving city of Indianapolis at last.

I made ready to put her down before we got too far into town. I didn't want there to be too much road traffic for what I had in mind.

As we descended, I came forward to look over the side and watch our progress.

"Why are you stopping here?" Henry asked.

I glared at him. "We should be well ahead of them, like you said. I mean to land beside the road here where there are no people and wait in ambush for them with the rifle."

"I'm not sure they will stop and give up at the mere sight of you holding a rifle."

"Would you rather I let you do it? You can add highway robber to your list of accomplishments."

He crossed his arms, then uncrossed them again.

"Theo, I—I have to tell you something. I've wanted to tell you for a while."

He covered my hand with his own, and in spite of myself I felt a distinct thrill, so I hurriedly knocked his hand away.

"You forget yourself, sir."

I didn't want to hear whatever it was he had to say.

I concentrated on flying, and soon I found a narrow place where dense trees grew up close to the road. I put down just beyond them. I loaded the carbine, and Henry made the ship fast with two ropes tied to trees.

"Set the switch to generate hydrogen so she'll be ready to go."

I pushed my goggles up on my head and rubbed my eyes. Taking up the gun in my arms, I walked out onto the road to wait.

"We don't have much wood left," Henry said.

"Be quiet. I'm listening for them."

"Maybe I can find some on the ground."

"Suit yourself."

The shadows stretched long on the road, and far away I could make out a distant huffing sound.

"Henry! They're coming. Where are you?"

I kept my eyes fixed on the road. The racer was moving fast. The sound it made was both higher-pitched and faster than the chug of a locomotive engine. I could tell they had the pressure way up.

Where was Henry? Why was he lurking out of sight somewhere behind the Kestrel instead of standing in the road helping me?

I shifted from foot to foot, wondering if they would be able to see me standing there in the middle of the dark paving in my blue flight jacket. I raised the rifle over my head and waved it back and forth. The racer roared up, the brakes screeched and the back end skidded out as they came to a stop.

The twins frowned at me, identical pouts on their rouged faces. They wore matching fitted blue silk jackets with straight cut blue sleeves. There was elaborate black frogging stitched on the wide collars, and white ruffled blouses peeped out around their necks. Their hats were ridiculous red rowboat-shaped affairs piled with silk loops in blue and black, and black and white feathers sticking straight out the back. With their goggles on, they looked like nothing so much as black and white crested long-necked birds.

I aimed the gun straight at them.

"Get out of the road, mademoiselle," one of them said. "We are in a rush."

"No. You have something of mine."

They looked at each other for a moment.

"Don't deny it," I said. "Just hand the vocalizer over, and I'll let you go."

The first one spoke to the other in French so rapidly that in spite of my years of studying French conversation, I could make neither heads nor tails of it.

"Que dites vous?" I asked.

They looked at one another and laughed in an infuriating way.

The other one said something—more French I could not understand.

"What are you saying to her?"

"That your French is atrocious and that you are bluffing."

She let go the brake and the monstrous machine surged forward, throwing out dust.

I flung myself out of the way. They lurched past me, then she slammed on the brakes again. I scrambled up from the roadway. To my horror, now that the roofless tender compartment in back was in view, I saw that the squint-eyed man had a long gun of his own held waist high and aimed straight at me. I tossed my carbine down and raised both my hands.

"All right, I give up. Keep the vocalizer."

The corners of the man's mouth curled up into an evil-looking smile and I heard a loud click as he cocked his weapon.

I heard peals of musical laughter, then a female voice shouting, "Tuez-la."

That French idiom was one I understood. It meant, *kill her.*

CHAPTER 11

SHOOT THE BREEZE

The man in the back of the racer raised his gun and took careful aim. I squeezed my eyes shut. I was knocked facedown onto the road at the same time the gun went off with a terrific report that hurt my ears. Through the ringing, I heard the racer's wheels spit gravel and roar off.

I'd been shot. I tried to move but something was pressing down on my legs. Oddly, there was no pain. Pushing up with my arms, I wriggled and looked back.

"Henry! Henry?"

He was splayed out on top of my calves, arms spread wide, unconscious.

"Henry, wake up." I twisted out from under him, knelt by his side, and put my hand on his shoulder.

He didn't move. Blood was dripping onto the ground from a wound somewhere on his head. I'd seen two dreadful injuries in one day, and it was simply too much. Tears rushed to my eyes.

"Henry, please, you have to be all right."

It didn't look good.

"Henry, can you hear me?"

He didn't move, so I turned him onto his back.

I looked closely at his head, but I couldn't see where the wound was. His hair on that side was soaked with blood. Parting his hair gently with my fingers, I was able to find the source of the bleeding.

It looked like the bullet hadn't gone in, but instead had just scraped a thin groove across his scalp on one side. I started breathing again. I checked him over, but could see no other injury.

I tore another piece off of my petticoat then sat down on the road and took his head in my lap. Pressing the wad of cloth against his head to stop the bleeding, my other hand cradling the side of his face, I listened to his breathing. It sounded deep and even, as though he were asleep.

"Please be all right," I murmured, stroking his cheek a little bit with my hand, tears still streaming down my cheeks.

He began to stir, and my heart picked up its pace. His dark lashes fluttered, then he opened his eyes. He looked up at me from where he lay in my lap.

"Lie still, you've been shot."

"I—what?"

"He shot you. In the head."

He reached up and his hand collided with mine.

"Be still. I'm holding a cloth on the wound to make it stop bleeding."

"There's a bullet in my head? How am I still alive?"

"It didn't go in, it scraped across your scalp. But it must have hit you hard enough to knock you out for a while."

"I'm all right, I think."

Little by little he sat up. I reached for his hand and guided it onto the makeshift dressing to hold it in place, and for some reason, I let my fingers linger on his a moment longer than I had to.

He met my eyes and little wry smile lifted the corners of his mouth. "How is it that your adventure is knocking the stuffing out of me, while you sit there pretty as a picture?"

A warm feeling started in my chest and rose upward to my face. Hastily I wiped my tears away with the back of my hand.

Then Henry got a look on his face as though he'd remembered something.

"You didn't get the vocalizer."

"No, I didn't." I frowned. "They laughed at me."

"Well they shouldn't have. You're very capable, you know."

"They knew I wouldn't shoot."

"Those twins are hard, ruthless women. And that man with the ugly eyes is even worse. You don't know what he might be capable of. I couldn't let him shoot you so I pushed you out of the way."

Sitting close to me like this, Henry's eyes were even darker and softer than I remembered, and I felt like I was getting lost looking into them.

"I can't believe you did that for me."

He took the cloth away from his head and looked at it, then touched the scrape with his fingertips.

"It's going to keep bleeding if you do that. Here, let me wrap it up."

I stood and tore more strips off of my petticoats. If he kept getting hurt at this rate, there would soon be nothing left of them. I wrapped the makeshift bandage around and around, feeling the warmth of his head in my hands.

"Better?"

He nodded. We both stood up and I took his arm to steady him.

"Thank you," he said.

I helped him aboard the aetherigible, then I quickly stoked the furnace, which had almost burned out. I busied myself with the boiler and switched on the hydrogen generator. Henry tried to help, but I thought he looked a little pale, so I made him sit in the front while I let the envelope fill so we could ascend. For once, he didn't give me any trouble.

"What are we going to do now?" Henry said.

"I'm going on to Chicago. I might not beat them there, but I know Mr. Quigley's address. If I can get the vocalizer back tomorrow morning, I still might have a chance."

"Are you sure that's the best plan? I got a good look at the racing carriage, and just like I thought, it had no light."

"What are you suggesting?"

"I think they'll stop for the night. It'll be dark in an hour or two. How many public houses can there be along the road? Why don't we go take a look and see if we can find them?"

"I don't know, I think I should find a doctor for you."

He put his hand on his head. "I'm not going to lie to you, it hurts and I'm a little dizzy. But I'm okay. I've had worse lumps. I think you should keep trying, and I want to help you."

A horse and carriage came clopping up the road at that point, and the driver pulled over to stop.

"Have an accident?" he called.

"Yes, but we'll be on our way soon."

The man tilted his head curiously to one side as he examined the Kestrel. "Say, what is that thing?"

"It's an aetherigible. A personal flying machine."

"I need to get one of those. All right then, as long as you folks are okay."

I waved, and the man went on his way.

"You know," Henry said, "I wondered where all the traffic was. I thought the National Road would be more heavily traveled."

"Tomorrow is market day. It'll no doubt be busier then."

I looked into the wood box, which was almost empty. Henry made as though to get up, but I waved him back.

"Stay here while I find some more wood."

Stepping into the dim woods, I soon found plenty of fallen branches to carry back. I asked Henry start chopping them to length while I went for more. Though he didn't complain, it seemed obvious to me his head was throbbing so I took pity on him and chopped them up myself.

I made one more trip and the wood box was full, and the envelope was close to being full too.

We had a little time before launch, and Henry looked ghastly with all that blood in his hair.

"Henry, would you let me rinse off the blood and change that bandage?"

He reached up and felt his hair, which was now stiff and spiky. "Do you think that would help?"

I shrugged. "At least you'll look better. I wish I had some carbolic acid, but this will have to do."

Uncle Adolphus had provided us with a bar of castile soap, so I took out a bucket and filled it from one of the ballast tanks. I unwound the bloody rags from his head.

"Bend over this bucket and dunk your head. I'll apply the soap."

Henry knelt down in the hull.

"I've never had a woman wash my hair before."

"Well don't get used to it."

"Ha."

He plunged his head into the water. I tried to remain businesslike, though I must confess, I was distracted. After I swished out the worst of the blood, he lifted his head up a little ways out of the water. I rubbed the soap in my two palms to bring up a lather, which I applied to his wound.

He flinched. "Thunderation and britches! That stings to high heaven!"

"There's no need to swear at me. I'm trying to help."

I tried to keep my hands gentle.

"Sorry," he said meekly, but his fingers clenched at the sides of the bucket.

"Dip your head back in and I'll rinse the soap away."

By the time I finished, my ministrations had opened the wound up again. I sighed and tore off yet more of my petticoats and bound his head back up. He stood, and I inspected the result.

"Well?" he said.

"You look much better. I think you'll have a scar, but your hair will cover it."

"Thank you."

Before that moment, I'd never taken care of another person before, and to hear his thanks made me feel a warm pride in the center of my chest. I'd been taking care of myself for so long that I had had little thought for others. I realized now how childish I'd been.

As I considered my new feelings, a sense of shame that I'd given Henry such a hard time before began to creep in. After all, his difficult circumstances had made him a thief, he hadn't sought it out. He'd been an exemplary crewman, tending the boiler, cooking, even taking a bullet meant for me. Perhaps there was some good in him after all.

The Kestrel was nearly buoyant enough to become airborne. I dumped the dirty water and bustled around, stowing things and generally tidying up. I took up Henry's jacket, which still bore white reminders of the morning's fiasco, and did my best to make it presentable. Feeling better, he busied himself tending the furnace and adjusting the boiler controls.

The magenta sides of the envelope began to swell, and we began rising into the air once again. My heart rose too. I thought I might have one more chance to accomplish what I'd set out to do.

The sun was coming down near the horizon, its beams peeking out from between the blue clouds drifting there. I pointed her west towards Indianapolis.

CHAPTER 12

SET A THIEF TO CATCH A THIEF

The sun was below the horizon and a glorious pink and orange glow spread through the gossamer clouds above our heads. We were flying low and fast, examining every public house or inn we happened across before the light gave out. So far, we'd found no trace of the racer.

"Henry, I've been thinking."

He turned his bandaged and goggled head to look back at me from his lookout spot in the prow.

"I want to apologize to you for the way I spoke to you before when you were talking about your grandmother. It was cruel, and I am ashamed I said it."

He shrugged. "I understand why you felt that way. The Ruffians are an appalling bunch. I thought you would put me aground after I told you, and you would've had good reason."

"I nearly did. But I was wrong. From what you told me, you're not one of them."

"You had a point, though. It's plain to me now, I have to find a way to get clear of them." He adjusted his goggles, a frown on his face.

We flew on into the gathering darkness, the only light now was from the lower edge of the sky in front of us.

"I don't think we're going to find them," I said. Time dragged slower and slower, and I could not see a way forward if we didn't find them before black night fell. I leaned back in my seat, tracing my fingers along the back rail and letting my eyes wander over distant farms and trees.

"Theo, come here!"

I jumped at the urgency in his voice and joined him at the front.

He pointed a ways ahead. There were occasional lights on the ground now, and I could faintly see a pale stone building with a tall copper dome and other signs of the city in the distance.

"Is that the state capital?" I asked.

"Not that. Look nearer to us. There, see the smoke?"

My goggles were limiting my vision, so I pushed them up onto my forehead. A thick column of white smoke rose close by the road next to a two story building. It looked like it might be steam.

"We need to get closer. But don't fly right overhead. Sidle up to it a bit," he said.

I loosened one valve to drop even lower, and steered to a point off to one side.

As we came closer, I knew we'd found our quarry.

Henry was leaning forward with one hand on the tether. "I think the engineer is venting the boiler. He'll put out the fire and clean out the firebox next. They're shutting down for the night."

I didn't answer. I was taking great care that I didn't overshoot them. All I needed was for Squinteye to spot us in the air.

Henry was taut with attention like a pointing dog. His head swung toward me again.

"It's a good thing we're flying out of the east. The sky is black behind us, and I doubt they can see us. Let's put down over there, well away from the inn."

When we were over the field he'd pointed out, I pulled the valves and set her down lightly into the grass, without a sound. We could barely see what was around us. Without the flickering flame from the boiler, it would be dark.

Henry dropped the ropes overboard. He leaped out, pressed stakes into the soft ground, and then tied her down front and back.

I switched the boiler over so she'd soon be floating and ready to go again, took up the carbine and climbed out.

"What are you doing?" Henry asked.

"I'm going to go get the vocalizer."

He got in front of me to block my way.

"It's far too dangerous. I can't let you take the risk. I know better than you what these people are capable of," he pointed to his head. "I don't want you to get hurt."

"I don't have a choice. You are hardly in any condition right now to march in and demand they hand it over." I gestured at his bandaged head.

He smiled a crooked smile. "You forget what my specialty is. I'll take a quiet look around and wait for a while, until I'm sure they've gone to sleep. Then I'll do what I know best. Besides, I'm expendable."

"Expendable," I snorted. "Where would it leave your grandmother if you went off and got yourself killed now?"

He grimaced.

"Please, Theo, let me do this for you. I'll find it and we'll be away before they even know it's gone."

I hesitated, and I could tell from his face in the glow from the firebox that he knew his argument was gaining ground.

He pressed his advantage. "You're the pilot and it's your aetherigible. Our best bet is to have you here at the controls so that she's ready to go the minute I get back."

"I don't know. That bump on the head might have addled your wits. Are you sure?"

"I'm fine. It'll be easy and fast. The simplest job in the world for an experienced thief," he smiled and put his hand on my shoulder reassuringly.

I didn't like it one bit, but his words made sense. Confronting them hadn't worked for me before. It stood to reason there was little chance it would work now. Reluctantly, I held out the carbine to him.

"No, I won't need that. I'll be stealing around in the dark, not marching in with a gun in my hands. You keep the Kestrel safe."

My heart pounded in my chest as I watched him walk away into the darkness. I am not a patient person. I threw another chunk of wood onto the fire and sat down anxiously in the pilot seat, the carbine in my lap.

The soft hoot of a great horned owl somehow reminded me of home, and my thoughts turned to Papa. Had he made it through the night? I had great faith in Dr. Jepson. He would not let Papa die. I clung to that.

My mind returned to the situation at hand, and peering into the darkness, I wondered what Henry was doing. Had he searched the racer? Was he creeping through a window at the inn? Or had he already been caught? I hadn't checked the time when he'd left, and I didn't know how long he'd been gone.

My human heartstrings were pulled taut in both directions.

I stared blindly into the darkness, striving my best to listen for the slightest sound of his return. I tapped my foot impatiently, and the owl went silent, only to start up again in a tree across the field a moment later.

Time dragged and my attention wavered. The night air cooled, and the crickets started singing. July was almost over and summer was getting on. I switched off the generator and vented a little hydrogen, not wanting the Kestrel to pull too hard on the stakes that secured her. Wrapping my coat more tightly around myself, I took out my timepiece to check the hour yet again.

Half past ten. How could he have been gone so long? Had something gone wrong and he'd been caught?

I had nearly made up my mind to go see, in fact, I had climbed over the rail and was standing there in the field, holding my carbine and dithering over what to do, when I heard voices in the distance.

I held still and listened.

The voices were low and indistinct, but I thought there were two of them. A shuttered lantern bobbed along, barely giving out any light.

I strained my ears, and heard the voices again. The tones were low, but strangely melodious, and one of them laughed.

They were speaking French.

I thought I could see two figures moving in the faint light of the lantern.

"Qui est-il?" I asked.

The familiar laughter burst out again. I was beginning to think my French wasn't what it ought to be. But they could at least have the courtesy not to laugh at my attempts. Papa always says that rudeness is something weak people engage in, but the twins' laughter had a real touch of meanness to it.

I raised my carbine to my shoulder and sighted along the barrel.

"I'm armed. Don't come any closer. I mean it."

More musical laughter rang out, and the lantern stopped. "Mademoiselle? Are you there with your ridiculous gun?"

"Where is Henry?"

"Why don't you come and see, mon petite? We have him here with us. And we have guns too."

"Henry?"

There was no answer.

"What have you done with him?"

"He is right here, don't you want to come see?" They laughed again.

I didn't answer. My hands trembled a little bit on the gun as I kept it pointed toward them, uncertain what to do.

"Drop your gun, and we'll give him to you."

I didn't answer.

One of them spoke again in French, the other answered, and they laughed together, a cruel sound.

"She doesn't want to come play with us," I heard one say.

"Show her," said the other.

The lantern shifted for a moment, and then the shutters opened and the light was directed toward two figures.

I could make out one of the twins close behind Henry. His arms were pulled behind his back and I could make out the white bandage on his head. His mouth was gagged and one of the twins had a pistol pointed at his head. I heard the sound of the hammer being cocked back.

I threw the carbine away into the darkness beside me.

"Let him go, I—"

Something hard clouted me above the ear and a dozen stars exploded in my head, then I knew no more.

CHAPTER 13

DEEPER IN TROUBLE

I dreamed—and the dream made no sense. I was lying under a thick, dark colored blanket, and I couldn't find my way out. I tried to open my eyes, but under the blanket I could not see. Voices mumbled somewhere in front of me in endless conversations, but I could not tell what they said. A snake slithered up and hissed in my face. Then a tiny locomotive approached, with a quiet chugging sound as it moved along its narrow tracks.

The back of my skull throbbed mightily as I came to and blinked my eyes. The moon was visible in the sky, shining from behind a screen of thin clouds.

I shifted my head to the side. Not far away, the light from the lantern shone out. I could see Henry lying on the ground. The man with the squinty eyes bent over him, doing something to his feet. Just behind them, the Kestrel bobbled at an obscene angle. Just one staked line still pinned her to the ground. The twins stood off to one side, speaking to one another in French.

I tried to move, but I couldn't. My hands were painfully bound behind my back. I could move my legs, but to no purpose. I struggled to sit up.

"Voila!" said one of the twins, noticing me in the light from the lantern. "Elle est éveillée."

"We are so glad you woke up, mademoiselle. We want you to see the fun we have planned."

I could see Henry struggling against his bonds, but he was trussed up like a chicken, and could not free himself. Squinteye tied one more loop around Henry's ankles and tested the knot by jerking up on it, causing Henry's feet to jump.

"He's ready," he said.

"Bon. Continue." The twins laughed, and the sound slid down my spine in a horrible way.

The man took out a large shiny knife, and bent toward Henry.

"NO!" I shouted.

"Oh, mademoiselle, you are so funny. The knife, it is not for him. See? It is for your silly toy airship."

Squinteye bent once again and began sawing at a rope. It gave way suddenly with a twang and the Kestrel slowly rose aloft.

"Here is—how do you say—the good part! Are you watching?"

As the airship kept rising, the coil of rope by Henry's feet fed out and up until he was suddenly jerked into the air. He swung back and forth, upside down.

"So you see, mademoiselle, if God had intended man to fly, he would no doubt have given him wings!"

Squinteye knelt down to put one hand on my back and began whispering breathily in my ear, sending an icy chill down my spine.

"You know, it's really a shame I don't have time to take care of you right. You and I could have so much fun together."

His hand slid down my back and I stiffened.

"Alas, the twins are eager to go, and I must obey. Maybe next time, my lamb." He brought his face closer still.

I shuddered and turned my face away to avoid his mouth, and saw Henry rotating slowly, his pale face contorted with anger behind the gag, wriggling violently to try to get loose of his bonds.

One of the twins spoke sharply. Their laughter rang out again, and the man picked up the lantern. They all strode away, leaving me sitting there.

My heart pounded in my chest.

By the stark white light of the moon, I could see the Kestrel rising sluggishly into the dark sky, her envelope not yet full enough to float straight. She was maybe thirty feet in the air with Henry hanging upside down underneath her.

I wriggled and pulled on the bonds around my wrists, but the cord was painfully tight. I bent my legs underneath me and after much effort, managed to rise to my feet.

"Henry! They tied my hands. You have to get yourself loose!"

He squirmed wildly on the end of his rope.

The night air shifted gently, and the Kestrel began to drift sideways, still rising slowly.

"Henry!"

Hands tight behind my back, I ran after him as best I could. After only a few steps, something caught my toe and I crashed to the ground, hitting my face. It hurt, but I paid no attention because when I fell, the cord burst from my hands. Squinteye must have been distracted when he tied the knot. Hastily I untangled the loops.

By this time the underinflated Kestrel had glided silently across the field. The airship—along with Henry—had come to rest against the branches of a tall tree.

I clambered up again, stumbled over to the tree and stopped, gazing up at him where he still struggled in the dim white light from the moon.

"Henry, hold still. You'll knock her loose."

My head was dizzy and my hands trembled uncontrollably. I was afraid to climb up, not only because of my unsteadiness, but also because I feared I might jar the Kestrel free from the branch and he would float away and disappear into the sky forever.

I staggered back to where I'd been when Squinteye had knocked me out. I groped around in the dark grass and before long I felt the long cold metal of my carbine under my hands.

Striding back over to the tree, I saw in the shadows that the envelope was almost full, and the Kestrel was beginning to lift up and would soon be free from the tree.

My brain worked furiously, but my options were limited.

I had to bring the Kestrel down. If I was very careful not to hit anything metal on the airship, there shouldn't be a spark to ignite the gas.

I hoped.

So I took aim and shot the top of the envelope.

With a hiss of gas, the envelope quickly began to lose its shape. The sinking keel hit the end of a branch and snapped it. I threw down the carbine. I got beneath Henry, ready to catch him.

Free of the branch, the hull sped to the ground. As Henry dropped I snatched at his shoulders to try to heave him out of the way, but his weight was too much and I tumbled backwards. Henry's bundled form landed square on top of me. All of my breath flew out of me.

The aft end of the hull crashed into the ground, then the front slammed down, narrowly missing us.

I lay there for a while stunned, unable to breathe, and then at last I took in a great gulp of air. Henry made some sounds behind his gag and wriggled.

I shoved him off to one side and gasped. He wriggled some more.

"Oh be still. I'll untie you in a moment. For pity's sake, let me catch my breath." I panted, my hand on my chest.

He let loose with a long stream of gagged vowels, none of which I could understand.

"All right, then, let me get a light. The moon's gone behind the clouds."

I fished a lantern out of the forward storage cupboard and lit it. "Hold still."

I started in on the rope around his hands and body. It took me some time to pick the knots apart. Once I'd freed his hands he snatched the cloth gag from his mouth and twisted around to look behind him. The Kestrel sat flat on the ground, her envelope sagging limply over her frame.

"Your aetherigible...," Henry said.

"I had to do it. A bullet hole was the only way I could think of to get you down. Are you all right?"

In the flickering light of the lantern, his eyes sought out mine.

"You did that for me?" he asked softly.

"I couldn't very well leave you dangling." I began untying his legs and feet.

"I have bad news," he said.

"I know, you didn't get the vocalizer."

"Worse than that. They have special lanterns."

"Special lanterns?" A great bubble of frustration rose in my chest. "What happened?"

"They were eating supper in the common room so I slipped into the bedrooms in the inn, but they were empty and I couldn't find anything. I was in the racer searching the tender when they came out to fit on the lanterns. That's when they caught me."

"You're saying they didn't stop for the night?"

He nodded his head. "I'm sure they've gone," he said.

My stomach turned queasy as I realized that even if I could fix the envelope, I might never catch them in the dark.

I wanted to give up, I did. I wanted to go home, to know whether Papa had woken up or not, to stop this fool's errand and return to my quiet life.

But I just couldn't. The invention was Papa's, not Mr. Quigley's, and I still meant to get it back. Though I was tired and frustrated and—yes, I'll admit it—frightened, I knew I would never be able to live with myself if I just stood by and let Papa be ruined merely because retrieving the vocalizer was proving to be too hard. I would not abandon my hope.

I would go on. My resolve calmed me, and all my fears and jitters disappeared.

Henry followed me over to the aetherigible. Without speaking, I quickly damped the furnace, which had almost burned out anyway.

The fall didn't appear to have hurt the hull. But my shot had gone cleanly through one side of the envelope and out the other, which was why the gas had escaped so quickly.

Uncle Adolphus predicted I'd need to patch the silk at some point, though this probably wasn't the reason he'd had in mind. I began rummaging around in the supplies he'd provided to find the cloth and rubber caulk.

Working silently beside me, Henry helped me apply the patches. It didn't look pretty, but soon enough we'd covered over the holes.

"I sure hope that holds." I twitched the envelope back into position and used the shovel to empty the ashes out of the firebox. Then I kindled the fire anew.

"What are you going to do now?" Henry said.

"I'm going on to Chicago. I might not beat them there, but I know Mr. Quigley's address. I will tell him what his people did to Papa and appeal to his sense of decency."

Henry frowned unhappily.

"I have to at least try. If I can get the vocalizer back from him tomorrow morning, we still might have a chance to get home in time." I looked at him.

Henry didn't say anything.

"You don't have to go with me."

"It's not that. Are you sure you want to do this? These people are dangerous. They thought it a great joke to hang me up by my toes, but they could just as easily have shot both of us."

"I am not afraid," I lied. "I'm going."

"Then I'll go with you."

He moved closer, his eyes soft and dark, and he took my hand in his, and the warmth of his grip reassured me.

Desire rose up in me, and in great confusion, I decided to pry his hand off of mine, but for some strange reason my limbs wouldn't follow the instruction from my head. My hand stayed right where it was, and he held it tight.

CHAPTER 14

WHAT IS PROPER, AND WHAT IS RIGHT

I had an idea where all this hand holding just might be headed. I must say, the thought had come into my mind before this moment of closeness happened that anything of that sort involving Henry was altogether impossible for a young lady like me. Completely impossible.

You see, I am not a complete stranger to the art of love. Back when I was still attending balls at the tender age of fifteen, I had many admirers.

The best of these, Mr. Ephraim Hall, was quite persistent. I didn't find him especially suitable, since he was rather short, and truth be told, had a tendency toward stoutness. He was very old—nearly thirty, though he carried himself like a much younger man.

The dinner was over and the gentlemen had retired apart from the ladies to the smoking room for cigars. My friend Amelia Goff had angered me in some way and I left the parlor where the young ladies had gathered. I cannot remember how—it might have been on a dare—Mr. Hall enticed me into the alcove by the stairs and I smoked his cigar.

In retrospect, it was a foolish thing to do, because the smoke drew the attention of Mrs. Goff, who had gone upstairs for some reason, and down she came to investigate. When her shrill voice sounded suddenly in my ear, I startled, and in doing so I tossed the cigar. With the worst possible sort of luck it landed right in her hair, catching her elaborate pile of curls on fire.

Pandemonium ensued, and Mr. Hall took me by the hand and helped me escape out onto the terrace. In a moment of enthusiasm, he placed his arm around my waist and kissed me.

I was irritated to be treated so. My feeling of delicacy was so shocked I had to stomp upon his shoe with my heel then bring my knee up sharply.

"Mr. Hall," I said, as he rolled on the terrace pavers, grasping his nether regions, "our friendship is at an end. Good night, Sir." I stomped home.

The worst part of all was that his kiss—my first—had not lived up to my expectation. I remember a distinct uncomfortable wetness and cold flabby clamminess to his fleshy lips, along with a stench of cigar smoke arising from the depths within. I would have preferred not to have been kissed at all, but the thing was done.

Suffice it to say, I gave him no opportunity to repeat the offence.

I made sure I didn't accidentally encourage any further gentlemen admirers after that night and through the years since.

Or at least I thought I didn't.

In spite of my attempts to keep our relationship businesslike, it seemed an affection had arisen between Henry and me, one I could not logically understand. He was entirely unsuitable for a girl of my station in society, and yet here I was by his side, letting him hold my hand and thinking about kisses.

The envelope stretched and reached the point of fullness, and with a whisper of long grass slipping along the hull, she lifted up smoothly and we took to the air.

The moon was still playing hide and seek between the clouds. A night breeze blew gently across our faces as we stood hand in hand in front of the boiler.

The fact was, I liked the way his warm fingers felt grasping mine.

I looked up into his face. As he looked back at me I saw an intensity in his dark eyes that I hadn't noticed before. It both frightened and thrilled me. How could I be awash in so many feelings simultaneously?

A little voice spoke in the back of my mind, telling me to think things through. I am impulsive, it is true. Papa chides me about it all the time. I often leap into situations without thinking. I think my impulsivity might be what makes me such a good inventor.

I told the little voice to be still.

I breathed deep and suddenly I caught his scent, the same warm, delicious smell I'd noticed when I'd climbed aboard the day before. A flood of warmth spread in my belly, and as my head swam, I found I could no longer sustain my better intentions.

"I don't give one whit about impossibility," I said.

"What?"

"Shhh."

I reached up and brushed my fingertip across his bandage and then put my hand through the hair on the back of his head, soft and silky to my touch. A distinct exhilaration ran through me as I gazed deeper into his eyes.

His hands went around my waist. It seemed the most natural thing in the world for me to pull him closer.

Our lips met, soft and gentle at first, then more and more urgently. A strange heat bloomed in me that I'd never felt before. It grew stronger and I leaned into him, shaping my body to his.

I had no idea kissing could feel like this.

Unlike Mr. Hall's lips, Henry's lips were warm and firm, yet soft and yielding at the same time. The contrast was positively dizzying.

I didn't want it to stop, but finally the kiss ended, and I stood with my hand on his chest, slightly dazed, though in the best possible way. I tried to catch my breath.

He tucked back a stray wisp of my hair, and the wind blew it forward again. He squeezed his eyes shut, then opened them again.

"Are you all right?" I asked.

He put one hand up to feel the bandaged side of his head. "Only a little lightheaded."

We stood silent for a time, and I cast about for something to say, but nothing would come to mind except a little niggling thought that would not go away. The little voice in the back of my head tried to warn me not to say anything, but the thought persisted, and finally I could hold it in no more.

"You must have had many lovers," I blurted.

A smile tugged at his lips. "No, I haven't. It is difficult to court a girl when you don't have any money."

"I must confess, I have been kissed one time before, but only the once. Does that matter to you?"

"Not in the least." He smiled again. "Miss Theodocia Hews, you are a caution."

"What do you mean, I am a caution? Was it something I said?"

"When two people are kissing," he said, putting his arms back around me again and speaking softly into my ear, "I believe the preference is that they say nothing at all."

His warm lips brushed my ear. My heartbeat sped up and a shiver of pleasure went through me.

I turned my face up to his and closed my eyes. His lips met mine, and we kissed again. My arms went around his neck, and I forgot everything else but him while we drifted through the pale silvery light of the cloud-rimmed night sky. I felt certain the romance of my life had commenced in earnest.

As we gained altitude, the moon went behind the clouds again, and the wind picked up and whipped at our clothes, though we hardly noticed. When finally I felt an especially strong gust lift the back edge of my skirt, I gently took my lips away from his.

"We're getting too high. I must turn off the generator so we can level off."

Pulling my hand from his, I slipped behind the boiler to work the switch. I wished I could tell Julia about Henry. She does so love to talk about romance. A smile played around my lips.

Then Henry's voice pulled me out of my reverie.

"Theo, come see!"

I went back to where he stood and took up his hand again. We were nearly over the Indiana State Capital Building. Newly built, it looked even more striking close up. Massive slabs of limestone formed the structure, and the dome reached high up into the sky. Lights shone out from the windows.

"It's beautiful," I said. "This is where we turn north."

"Looks like it's clouding over." He indicated the gathering darkness overhead. "Without the moon, how will you know where to steer?"

"I will just put the wind on my left cheek and pray that it doesn't shift direction."

"You know, that's something I like about you," said Henry.

"What?" I asked, feeling pleased to hear him say those words.

"You always have a plan."

Considering the complex ambiguousness that was my future with him, I thought to myself that he couldn't be more wrong.

But I had one goal on which to focus for now. Reaching Chicago. I checked over the controls and made a minor adjustment to our direction.

Henry pulled on his goggles to protect his eyes from the wind, and stepped up to the front of the hull, grinning.

"What's so funny?" I asked.

"Oh, nothing. Sometimes a fellow just feels like smiling."

I pondered this. Usually what men thought was a source of mystery to me, but in this instance I thought I could understand what he meant. I was smiling too.

He reached up and took hold of one of the tethers.

"The only thing that would make this night more perfect would be a good cigar," he said.

"Well, I'm happy you don't have one. My past experience suggests tobacco is bad for the hair."

He whistled a little tune for a while, and then came back to where I sat in the pilot's seat.

"You've taken the entire burden of steering on this trip. May I help?"

"It's kind of you to offer, but you don't know how."

"I did have the tiller when the Kestrel first left your roof," he reminded me.

"The propeller wasn't even engaged. I would hardly count those few seconds you sat in the chair before I took control as experience flying an airship."

"Well I have held the string of a kite, how much harder could it be?"

I looked at him. "You're teasing me again, aren't you?"

He grinned again. "Maybe just a little bit. But if you're tired, I'd be happy to let you have a rest. And I mean that sincerely."

"I am quite wide awake, thank you very much."

I was not certain why, given our new affection for one another, but his offer annoyed me a bit. Even if we were now friends or perhaps more than friends, the Kestrel was mine.

He went forward and lay down, pulling out a sack of potatoes upon which to rest his head. He stretched out and put his arms behind his head.

"Whatever are you doing?" I asked.

"Well, if you're not going to let me steer, I've had a full day taking a beating for our cause, and a man must go to bed sometime."

He hummed a happy tune for a while, and then he quieted. He had fallen asleep.

I gazed at him for a long time. His long dark lashes lay thick on his cheeks. His jaw was square and firm and his skin was smooth like a bolt of fine cloth. I longed to run my fingertips along his face, but I stayed where I was. As he breathed in and out, his chest rose and fell peacefully, and his hair tousled gently in the wind.

Smiling, I went back to the pilot's seat and set my goggles over my eyes. I had intended to fly as straight toward Chicago as I could relying on dead reckoning, but the night was dark, and lights from the ground would be few and far between once we passed beyond Indianapolis.

At that point in time I had a stroke of luck, my first real luck since we'd left my uncle's farm. As I passed over the rail yard north of Indy, a freight train pulled onto the main track on its night run to Chicago. I lined up over the engine's running lights and smoke stack.

I held my breath as the locomotive got up to speed. Would I be able to match it?

The engine was hauling a long train of boxcars. They stretched away back into the distance, obviously heavy and full. I could just barely see the smoke puffing out of the smokestack from the lights on the front of the engine and the glow of coal burning in its huge firebox.

I adjusted the pressure of my boiler almost to maximum. The Kestrel was keeping pace. The idea that this part of my journey might be easier than what came before made me beam with pleasure, and I sat back in my chair to relive my kiss with Henry. It seemed strange to me that such a simple thing as two people pressing their lips together should cause such a tumult of feelings and sensations. I touched my fingertips to my mouth and nearly decided to wake him, but then I remembered he'd had a difficult day and had earned his rest, so I let him sleep.

My mind drifted home, and I realized with a start it had been hours since I'd even thought about Papa. Worry slipped into my mind. I wondered how he was. Had he improved, or was he still unconscious abed? I knew Dr. Jepson would stay by his side, but still, I felt terrible that I hadn't yet managed to get the vocalizer and return home.

Even worse, what if he was awake and reading the note I'd left for him? He would certainly be worried now that I'd been gone for two days. I've given my father loads of reasons in the past to be concerned about me, but nothing came close to this trip I'd undertaken. My eyes darted around and came to rest on Henry's sleeping figure. My worry changed over to guilt over what I'd just done, however sweet the impulse had been.

I sighed and shook myself mentally. It wouldn't do to worry or feel guilty. I had made up my mind, and I could deal with Papa once I returned. The wind was picking up, so I pulled my coat collar tight around my neck. I adjusted my goggles and settled in for a long night, determined not to fall asleep this time.

CHAPTER 15

THE LULL BEFORE THE STORM

I stoked the fire from time to time but otherwise I stayed in the pilot's seat. I flew on for several hours in that manner, managing to keep up with the freight train below thanks to its habit of slowing down and blasting its steam whistle for crossings and stopping once in a while for water.

The wind was now blowing stronger than before, and it became harder and harder to keep the Kestrel on a steady heading. My arm and wrist were growing stiff from fighting the wind's pulls against the tiller.

The ride was getting rougher. I couldn't believe Henry was sleeping through it all. I began to worry a bit about the unseen damage the bullet had done to his head, glancing though the blow may have been. A series of strong gusts rocked the airship sideways. I fixed the tiller in place and made my way around the boiler to the front.

"Henry, wake up."

He didn't answer. He was sound asleep.

"Henry?"

I went to him, grasped his shoulder, and gave it a little shake.

"Must you wake a fellow in the middle of the night?" He reached up to put his arms around me and pulled me down onto him. "I was having such a vivid dream."

"Henry—"

"Mmm, I know, we shouldn't. It isn't proper and all that—"

He brushed his lips across my cheek.

"True, but no, I—"

A huge bolt of lightning split the sky, followed by thunder so loud it shook my bones.

Henry lurched upright, shoving me unceremoniously to one side. "What the devil? Is it storming?"

For all his mechanical ability, Henry sometimes had a tendency to state the obvious. A violent wind gust punched into the envelope, sending us skidding sideways in the sky.

"That's why I was trying to wake you."

"I'm sorry I laid hands on you."

He eyed the black sky up above. The intermittent lightning was the only way to make out any feature of the clouds in the blackness.

"Don't you think we'd better go down?" he said. "That lightning could make the gas explode."

"I—I'm not sure. We probably should, but if we do, I'll lose the train that I've been following, and we would have to wait until morning to take to the air again. The storm isn't that close yet."

As if in answer, a bolt of lightning ripped to the ground four or five miles from our position. Henry jumped as though he'd been stuck with a pocketknife.

Then an odd thing happened. Lightning formed a giant, jagged ring in the sky around my airship without touching it. The circle shimmered and glowed up there in the air for a moment, making a faint, silvery ringing sound as the wind blew us clear through it. Then it disappeared without ever touching us or the ground.

Strangely, there was no accompanying clap of thunder. Goose flesh rose on the back of my neck, and a strange tingling spread out in the very top of my head and in my fingertips. When I looked over at Henry he was scrutinizing at his own hands, spreading his fingers then turning them over to examine his palms. His hair stood up on his head.

"What was that?" he yelled.

A peculiar wild excitement filled me, yet I didn't answer. I looked up into the sky just as another flash lit up the inside of the cloud.

I had recently read a series of interesting articles on the nature of electric plasma theorizing the use of electricity to power large and small devices. When I got back, I really needed to conduct some experiments of my own. But for now I had to shake the strange electric thrill and focus on keeping up with the train.

"Theo?" Henry shouted.

I've often been told that stubbornness is not one of my better qualities, but I didn't want to give up the chase just yet even if he wasn't entirely comfortable with the electricity in the air. I had to yell to be heard over the howling of the wind. "Perhaps the storm will pass around us."

Henry stood at the gunwale clinging to a tether, scanning the sky. In the brief flashes of white electrical light, I could see the storm stretched from north to south and was coming for us in a great wall of roiling black clouds that twisted and turned like a bucketful of water snakes.

"I don't think so. Be reasonable."

This last bit involuntarily raised my hackles. My entire life, I have listened to one adult after another trying to mold my moral character by entreating me to 'be reasonable.' Could they not admit just once that I sometimes had a point?

I crossed my arms over my chest.

"We can fly a little longer. The heart of the storm is still miles off."

Another bolt of lightning split the sky. Henry cringed.

"It's terrifying up here! Come on, it will take us a while to get down anyway in all this wind."

"But the train..." I trailed off.

I frowned and looked down for its lights. The engine had pulled a substantial distance ahead, because the Kestrel was losing speed from having to fight against the gusts of wind. I hated to admit it—though I'd already known it myself when I woke him up to begin with—sooner or later, we had to land.

"Trim those tethers, they've stretched." I pulled two of the gas release valves.

For an eerie moment or two all the tiny hairs on my arms felt like they were standing on end, then a huge, multi-forked bolt of lightning blasted from cloud to ground practically beside us. The thunder was instantaneous and deafening.

Henry threw himself over me and we huddled together in the bottom of the ship as the thunder rolled on and on.

Obviously, I'd made an error estimating when the business end of the storm would arrive, and clearly I'd been foolish to imagine I could eke out a little more distance.

I raised my head cautiously.

"Empty the ballast," I shouted.

We needed to descend fast. One bolt like that to our envelope, and we'd go up in a great ball of flaming hydrogen.

Henry opened the drains and began pumping the water out when it didn't flow fast enough to suit him. I pulled the rest of the valves open, and we plummeted, rocked back and forth and blasted in an easterly direction by the powerful winds.

I realized we were dropping with stomach wrenching speed.

"Henry, don't pump so fast!"

Either he couldn't hear me or he wouldn't stop.

I tried to recap some of the envelope valves.

By this time, the sides of the envelope were rippling in the wind as we plunged downwards. I doubted she had much buoyancy left at all. The only thing keeping us up was that sideways wind.

"We're going to hit hard!" Henry yelled.

I took to my seat, stubbornly clinging to the tiller. Lightning flashed left and right.

"Get down in the center of the hull!" Henry yelled.

When I didn't respond, he grabbed my arm and pulled me past the boiler and down to the floor. We smashed into the ground with such force it slammed our bodies against the wood underneath us then bounced us up again for a second.

But the wind wasn't finished with us. Even though nearly all of the gas was gone, the metal frame kept the envelope up and it acted like a sail, dragging us sideways.

The rain began pouring from the clouds, and we were both instantly drenched. The lightning kept striking all around us.

"There's a cow shed over there," Henry yelled.

"I don't want to leave her, she'll blow away."

"There's nothing in this empty field to tie her to." He grasped both of my wrists and pulled me upright. "We have to leave now, or we'll be killed by lightning."

He helped me wrench my heavy, wet skirts over the side, and we stumbled through the streaming sheets of rain and dark toward the cow shed, correcting course whenever the flashes of lightning showed us the way.

We plunged through the opening in the side of the shed, disturbing four or five cows huddled inside. Since the shed had no door, we felt our way around the inside to a far corner, much to the dismay of the cows, who mooed suspiciously and shifted themselves toward the opening.

I've never been one to particularly enjoy the company of livestock. The wet cows stank, and the muck on the floor of the shed stank worse, so that we didn't dare sit down. There was a fine mist of rain blowing inside, in spite of the fact that the side with the opening was out of the wind. I reached up to touch my hair and found it flopping to my shoulders quite unbound, so I set about plucking out the remaining pins to put them into my pocket. Somehow I'd lost my goggles.

In the flashes of lightning, I could see Henry's face rigidly staring out into the darkness.

"Do storms trouble you?" I asked him over the loud drum of rain on the roof.

"I'm not fond of them," he admitted, pushing a cow aside to stand closer to me.

"This is a miserable night," I said.

He didn't answer. Lightning struck close by—so bright I blinked my eyes. The impact of the bolt hitting the ground jarred the soles of my feet. One of the cows gave a low bellow.

With the next flash, I could see Henry's eyes were wide with fear. I reached my hand up to touch his face, and he flinched.

"Don't be afraid, it'll pass soon."

"I'm not afraid," he grumbled.

But I could tell he was. I put my arm around his waist, but he pulled away from me. I tried not to crowd him, and I wondered what had happened to him in his childhood to make him feel that way about bad weather.

I've never been one to fear a storm. In fact, as a child, I'd often climb out of bed and watch the lightning from nighttime storms passing outside my window. I thought the blue-white electricity tracing its way across the sky was exciting and beautiful. But I suspect if I hadn't had a nice snug house in which to live and my strong Papa in his room across the hall, I might not have felt that way.

Henry stood still and rigid in the dark, and I felt a tender sort of protectiveness. I didn't press him about his fear, but instead just continued to keep my silence in hopes my presence comforted him.

The lightning strikes began to look dimmer and farther away, and the thunder quieted. Except for distant flashes, the night was now truly black as pitch, and I wished I'd thought to grab a lantern before we'd fled the Kestrel. The cattle shifted from foot to foot over on their side of the shed. My worry grew as the rain pattered more gently now on the roof.

"Should we go see what's left of her?" I asked.

A flash of lightning lit up Henry's face and he cleared his throat. "It's still raining."

"Yes, but we're already sopping wet. Come on." I led the way out into the drizzle. Henry grunted and followed after me as I set off in the direction we'd come.

The lightning was still flashing faintly in the distance, though the thunder was slow to follow and only grumbled quietly. At one point we stumbled into a rivulet caused no doubt by the downpour, but I wasn't sorry about the water flowing over our shoes after the mucky wait in the cow shed.

The rain let up as we plodded along in the dark. Finally, after slogging around blindly for a while, we reached the Kestrel.

Henry fumbled around in the blackness until he found a lantern in the cupboard. The glass was cracked but it still held its kerosene. Henry struggled to light it with the damp wooden matches, patiently striking them over and over.

As I watched and waited, the tiny spark flared and he managed to light the wick. The warm light glowed forth.

The lantern's flickering light confirmed my worst fears. My airship had been dragged by the wind the whole length of the field until she'd snagged on some bushes near the fence. The envelope was empty and dangled limply over the frame off to one side. There was a long tear where the wind had whipped it against the metal. We unhooked the tethers and pulled the wet silk off.

Standing there shivering, holding the bedraggled envelope in my hands, the weight of the task I'd undertaken overwhelmed me.

Everything I'd tried to do to get the vocalizer back, every step I'd taken, every last bit of it had gone wrong. The vocalizer was probably in Chicago already, and I was no closer to getting it back than when I'd started. A painful lump formed in my throat, and I sank down onto the deck, my wet skirts puddled around me.

Henry was instantly there at my side, touching my arm as my shoulders heaved.

"I can't do it...it's hopeless."

Henry slid his arm around me.

"Why did I ever think I could get it back? I can't do it. It's too hard," I snapped angrily.

Henry patted my back. "Don't say that."

"No, it's true. I'll never get there."

"Who invented this aetherigible? You did. And it's pure genius. You've just had a little bit of bad luck with this storm. That's all. We still have the patching kit. We'll fix it."

I held my face in my hands as the tears flowed from my eyes, and images of crashing into the tree, the flock of pigeons, and that evil-eyed man shooting at us came into my mind. There'd been more than a little bit of bad luck in my journey. The only thing that had gone right was Henry being there, though I certainly hadn't thought that when the Kestrel looked like it would float away from the roof without me or when I'd found him sitting there in my seat.

"Henry? Why did you stay with me? This isn't your concern. Why didn't you jump ship that first morning?"

A funny, crooked little smile spread across his face. "I did jump ship."

"Well yes, but after that any reasonable person would have run as far from me and my aetherigible as they could. Why didn't you?"

He averted his eyes and rubbed at his nose. "I guess I felt like I owed it to you. To...set things right."

"Owed it to me? For the Kestrel getting you out of the grasp of those policemen? That doesn't make sense."

He shrugged his shoulders. "I'm here now. What can I do to help?"

I wiped my eyes with my wet sleeve, which did next to no good at all. "I guess we'd better get sewing. See if you can find the patches."

The job was difficult, there in the dark with only the light of a single lantern, but little by little we sewed up the rip and put on several patches. We ran out of sealing rubber halfway through, and I prayed that she would hold enough hydrogen to get aloft again. I didn't feel like I had any choice but go on.

If we didn't get her into the air, we'd have a long walk to find some farmer to take us to a train station.

As I put on the finishing touches, Henry managed to get a fire lit in the furnace, and miraculously, the gas generator still seemed to be working even after the rough landing we'd had.

"I'm going to start a fire on the ground so we can dry off while we wait for her to fill," Henry said, setting out a box for me to sit on. He began rummaging around under the bushes.

"Hey, look. Your goggles! They must have fallen out when the ship caught on this brush."

My spirits rose considerably and I polished the glass lenses with my sleeve then set about pinning up my hair and placing the goggles on my head.

Henry quickly gathered an armload of wood that didn't seem quite so wet and kindled a fire. We draped our coats over nearby bushes to dry.

After a while, Henry scraped some coals from the fire and began frying bacon and potatoes. As I breathed in the delicious aroma, my spirits began to rise again.

"That smells lovely. Where did you learn to cook so well?"

"There wasn't anyone else to do it when granny got sick. I burned the food the first few times, but I learned quickly enough after that. There's not that much to it."

I thought of Emmoline and how she'd taken over the cooking duties when we'd had to fire the cook and our other staff. She'd never complained one bit, and her meals were always tasty, though sometimes there wasn't much food in our pantry for her to cook.

I needed to do better appreciating all she did for us.

The bacon was hot and crisp and the potatoes were golden brown and perfectly fried. My mouth watered as I took the first bite.

"I wish we had some eggs," he said.

"We haven't had eggs at our house very often in the past months." I shoveled in another bite in a most unladylike way.

"We have them all the time. They're one of the easiest foods to come by—er, to cook. You know, you aren't at all what I thought you were when I saw you there in the market with your fancy dress and hat."

"Even though it has been trying at times over the past months, Papa says we must keep up appearances," I shrugged nonchalantly. "Anyway, when I get the vocalizer back and Papa gets paid for it, all of our difficulties will be over."

Henry stirred the coals thoughtfully. "Well you and your father are far above me, that's for sure."

He didn't seem to be teasing this time. I wondered if he was right. Maybe I put on airs sometimes because I grew up on Mount Belvedere, but the truth was, we were only one step away from being turned out of our house. Perhaps I'd been wrong to think of myself as being so far above him. He did torment me awfully, but he was also kind and gentle and helpful.

I finished my food and began putting things away aboard the Kestrel. A good hot meal in my belly, and I found my determination had returned.

CHAPTER 16

IF THE TRUTH WERE KNOWN

Waiting for the envelope to fill this time was slow agony. Visions of the twins handing over the vocalizer to their employer spun through my head from time to time and my determination began to shift to anger. How dare they take what was not theirs? This time, I wouldn't hesitate to use the carbine to warn them off if I had to. I would take the vocalizer back to Papa no matter what.

While Henry was acting in an outwardly kind and helpful manner, I was, however, beginning to suspect that something had gone strange between us after I'd woken him up in the bottom of the hull. I thought the reason he hadn't kissed me in the cow shed was because of his fear for the storm, but I'd taken his hand a couple of times since then, and though we had nothing to do but wait for the envelope to fill while we sat by the fire, he hadn't so much as turned toward me.

He busied himself with little chores, hardly looking at me when I spoke.

I aimed to change that. When the envelope was nearly full and the first gleam of dawn filled the eastern horizon, I climbed aboard and crowded next to him where he stood at the rail. I was stunned when he actually moved away from me.

I placed my hand on his arm. "Are you going to tell me what's wrong, or am I going to have to torture it out of you with a hot iron?"

"What?"

What if I'd been mistaken about his affection for me? Had I misread the situation and forced it, and now he didn't want anything to do with me? But why had he pulled me down onto the floor with him when I woke him? None of it made any sense.

There was nothing for it but to lead him straight to the question.

"Before the storm, when we kissed, I—well, I thought...." I trailed off, unable to say the rest.

His face looked troubled in the glow of the lantern.

"Oh that. Since that near miss with the lightning, I—I've been thinking about it, and it was all wrong. I never should have taken advantage of you that way. It wasn't gentlemanly, not at all. Not that a thief could ever be considered a gentleman. But I'm all wrong for you and it never should have happened."

My mouth dropped open. It's a rare thing for me to be at a loss for words.

Henry dropped his gaze, unable to look at me, and continued. "I wasn't myself. That blow to the head made me dizzy, and I was pretty much exhausted. I'm sorry about what I did, and I promise I won't tell anyone. I don't want your reputation sullied."

I was stunned. What in the name of Sam Hill was going on here? Hadn't I been the one to start that first kiss? Didn't he understand that I wanted it to happen?

An awful thought struck me and a sickening sensation grew in my middle. What if he didn't care for me or my kisses at all? What if this was just his way of getting out of having to...I couldn't even complete such an awkward and embarrassing thought. I must be wholly undesirable to him, and a dreadful kisser to boot.

If this is what came of associating with men, this ghastly shame, then I would be better off forgetting anything ever happened. I straightened my shoulders, and went back to the pilot's chair to wait for liftoff.

◇◇◇◇◇◇

The Kestrel floated through the sky in the midst of a gray dawn. I steered her course by the railroad tracks below. We were in Illinois now, and wide fields of corn and wheat spread out below us. I had a vague idea the railway line I was following would end up at the Union Stockyard Gate, which I knew to be fairly close to downtown Chicago.

The farmhouses below were closer together now, and buildings clustered around the tracks here and there, marking small town stations. The tracks led onward.

Even from the height of seven hundred feet, I smelled the stockyards long before I saw them. As we drew closer, I saw a great brown scar cut into the land with nary a tree in sight. A vast spread of muddy pens full of hogs and cattle, all crowded together waiting to go to slaughter and stinking to high heaven stretched out below us. Wishing I'd thought to bring a scarf, I held one hand over my nose and turned the tiller sharply to head upwind.

I could now see Lake Michigan and the outlines of downtown Chicago. Approaching the city, it surprised me to see that even now, eight years after the Great Chicago Fire had finally been extinguished, evidence of the disaster was still plainly visible just like it had been the last time my father and I had flown over. Everywhere I looked, houses and commercial buildings were in various states of blackened desolation, active demolition, or new construction. Whenever I saw a building going up, it reminded me of the thousands of dollars in funds collected by the churches of greater Cincinnati after the fire. They were being put to good use.

I pointed the Kestrel toward the lakeshore, where I intended to land on whatever open space I could find and ask directions.

Through all this, Henry silently stoked the furnace whenever it ran low of fuel without my having to ask. When he was idle, he stood at the front rail looking out over the landscape, never meeting my eye. He said not a word, and I tried not to think about him. Instead I endeavored to keep my mind focused on what I'd set out to do.

I brought the Kestrel down and landed her right on the beach.

Henry leaped out and began driving the stakes into the ground to tie her down.

"Would you like me to find a carriage?" he asked.

"No, just stay here with the Kestrel and get her ready to relaunch. It shouldn't take me long to ask someone where Quigley's office building is."

Pulling the ticket out of my pocket, I strode off toward Lakeshore Drive, and flagged down a passing mailman.

"Excuse me, so sorry to interrupt you on your rounds, but could you tell me where this is?"

I showed him the address.

"I know the place. It's not far from here. Go six blocks further north, and then left eleven blocks. It's a new red brick building, you can't miss it."

I thanked him and walked back over to the Kestrel. She'd filled quickly and was ready to go, like a dog ready to hunt, and I felt a thrill as I took to the air again. I was close this time. I could feel it.

It only took a few minutes to reach the new home of Quigley Enterprises near the Chicago River. I held position over it for a moment to learn the layout. The building was newly completed with a squat, ill-favored design. The grandiose face of it had the ugly look of cheap construction.

Traffic was busy on nearby Wacker Drive, so I looked for a more likely place to set her down. My heart began thudding in my chest. The lot directly behind the Quigley building was empty, so I landed there and readied myself to confront Mr. Quigley himself.

Since I was in the city, I decided to leave the carbine behind.

Henry looked directly at me, his eyes piercing me. "Are you sure you want to do this? It might be dangerous."

"I am going in the front door of a business. What are they going to do? Shoot me in broad daylight with all those people passing by?"

"I only think that—"

I interrupted him before he could tell me what he thought. "I will see this thing finished. If you want to help me, stay here with my aetherigible and keep it safe."

"Theo, please—"

I spun on my heel and walked away without listening. He could go hang for all I cared.

Mr. Quigley was a businessman and surely he would behave honorably when he found out what his employees had done. He might not even be aware of their actions. It was Thursday morning, and with or without Henry's help, I would soon have the vocalizer in my hands and be in the air and on my way back to Cincinnati.

In a flash I was around the corner and standing on the threshold, but before I could pull on the handle, the door swung open right in front of me and a tall elegant man wearing a golden topcoat and an ornately figured, dark yellow silk vest bumped into me sending me rocking back onto my heels. He swept off his matching top hat.

"My apologies, my dear young woman, I did not see you there. Have I startled you?" His southern accent was slow and thick as honey, and he placed a light hand on my upper arm to steady me.

"Fine, thank you," I said, flustered.

He let go of my arm and his eyes slid up to my hair then down my figure, lingering on my wrinkled hem and dirty ankles. "Why, I declare, you look to have had a difficult morning."

"You don't know the half of it."

With a flourish, he held the door for me.

I thanked him and stepped through without looking back, though I could feel the sensation of his eyes on the back of my skirt for a few moments longer until the door closed again with a gentle thump. An accent like that was a rare thing to hear in the Midwest, but I didn't give it another thought. Instead, I straightened my shoulders and looked around the entry hall.

A clerk with greased-back hair wearing a cheap vest and shirtsleeves sat at an oak desk near the stair. He did not rise. Apparently his employer didn't set much store by good manners. I walked straight up to him, putting on my best professional manner.

"I am here to see Mr. Quigley."

The clerk looked at me impassively. "Have you an appointment?"

"No, but I insist upon seeing him right away."

The clerk leafed through the pages of the appointment book in front of him, then fixed me with a doubtful eye. "Mr. Quigley is not available."

I frowned. "What do you mean? He isn't here?"

The clerk scowled back at me. "That's not what I said. Mr. Quigley is a busy man, and he does not make time for just any little ragamuffin who walks in the door."

I looked down at my rain bedraggled flight jacket and skirts and caught the odor of my manure-stained boots.

I felt my face go hot.

"Sir, appearances notwithstanding, I have urgent business with Mr. Quigley concerning the Orin Hews Remote Vocalizer, and I demand to see him immediately."

A voice floated lazily down the stairs. "It's all right, Parker, I can see her now."

A mustachioed, bald-headed man dressed in a tailored but tasteless brown suit stood at the top of the stair, peering at a heavy gold pocket watch in his hand. He snapped it shut and beckoned to me, and I hitched my skirts and climbed up to him with as much dignity as I could muster in my crumpled clothes. He stood at an open door and waved me in, pulling out a seat for me.

"I prefer to stand." I stood rigidly erect, my head held high.

"Suit yourself," he said. "And you are?"

"Theodocia Hews."

He smiled an oily smile.

"Let me guess, you must be Orin Hews' daughter. How delightful of you to come visit me."

I looked about his office, which was furnished with an imitation mahogany desk and bookcases untidily stuffed with papers and unusual gadgets. On his desk, in an elaborate gilt frame, sat a photograph of the twins dressed in matching striped skirts. Taking in the simpering looks on their faces in the picture, I saw red. He noticed my expression.

"Do you like the photograph? Aren't my two protégées something?" He touched the frame, amusement twisting his lips.

I scowled. "Mr. Quigley, I will get straight to the point. Last week, you sent the twins to renew your offer for my father's invention, and he rejected your proposition all over again. Though I'm sure you had no knowledge of it, they then decided to take the vocalizer by force."

Mr. Quigley stood silently behind his desk with his fingertips resting on its surface, his face a mask.

I plunged on. "Your employees brutally attacked my father, leaving him gravely injured, and stole the device. They then transported it here by means of your racing carriage. I know you have it, and you will return it to me at once."

He folded his arms and smiled a menacing smile. "Wrong."

"Wrong? You lie, sir. I know you have it. You will give it to me this instant, or I will call in the police."

He reached forward to touch the picture frame once again. "They are so talented—and in so many different ways. Usually when I send them out they return straight away with the invention in their delicate hands and the patent tucked safely away inside one or the other corset. I must say I was shocked that a lonely man like your father was able to resist their considerable charms not once, but twice." He stroked his moustache, an ugly habit.

"My father isn't lonely," I growled. "Mr. Quigley—"

"It wasn't transported by racing carriage. I brought it back myself on the Peregrine on Tuesday, then sent it on."

"You—you—" I could not get the words out.

"Take your time, my dear," said the odious man.

"You admit it?"

"Of course. I thought your father might come after it in the airship he built on the roof of your house—"

My head was hot with rage. "It's not my father's, it is *my* aetherigible, *my* secret invention."

His face split in a smile of delight. "Your invention? How marvelous! So your father doesn't know you've come to Chicago."

I didn't respond.

He laughed, then shook his head and fixed me with eyes like a hound dog. "My dear, do you think it's proper for a young lady to go gadding about with a man unchaperoned?"

My face flushed anew. How could he know I had flown to Chicago with a man?

"I hired the one of the Ruffians to sabotage the airship, but the man seems to have botched it up, though he did buy me enough time to get the device off to my manufacturer."

The Ruffian?

My head spun dizzily with images that suddenly made ghastly sense. Henry the thief on the roof, stealing the Kestrel, shocked at seeing me climb aboard. He'd let me fall asleep, and probably damped out the fire in the furnace so we'd drift off course. He'd gleefully smashed the ballast tanks, nearly destroying the platform.

At my uncle's workshop, he'd insisted on redesigning the steering fins in a way that did nothing to help her fly better. That afternoon he'd urged me to tack, losing precious time so that I missed the departure of the racer in Dayton. He gave no warning when we encountered the flock of pigeons, though he surely must have seen them from his place up front, then he kept me distracted until we floated well out of sight of the road below.

He told me his sad story—probably all lies—to get my sympathy and gain my trust. He kept asking to take the tiller, no doubt intending to put us off course, but I hadn't fallen for it. He pretended to be afraid of the lightning, urging me to land instead of sticking with the freight train.

He'd tried to delay or confuse me at every turn. Even Uncle Adolphus had tried to warn me, but I did not listen.

How could I have been so blind?

"You're not saying anything, my dear. Did my hired man do anything—untoward?"

Judging from the heat radiating outward, I was certain my face had turned an even brighter shade of crimson. And Mr. Quigley—that cheap, ugly man—pulled out his chair, took his seat, and began to hoot and chortle at me until tears squeezed out of the corners of his eyes.

"Ho ho ho," he laughed. "Ha ha. It is just too delicious. Has the handsome rogue had his way with you up there in the sky in the dark of the night? To think, high and mighty Orin Hews' daughter, spoiled by a member of the Ruffian gang!"

He laughed raucously and took out a dirty handkerchief and wiped his eyes.

It had only been a kiss, nothing more. I passed from shame back into anger. I hate a false accusation worse than anything, there is no integrity in it, no fair play. I mastered myself, and eyed him coolly.

"You are mistaken, sir."

"Oh really? The details hardly matter when your father and the rest of Cincinnati society learn of the circumstances of your little three-day pleasure jaunt north." He took another swipe at his eyes with the handkerchief and stroked down his moustache again with his fingers, smiling all the while.

I stepped up to his desk in a cold fury and held out my hand.

"You have the vocalizer. Give it to me now."

"Can't. I told you before, it's already gone on to my manufacturer. But you were so kind to come by to see me. Please do visit me again whenever you like. I'm sure I can show you a better time than that young scoundrel. I do so enjoy the company of young women." He stood up and leered at me, reaching for my hand.

I yanked it back before he could touch it. "I am going straight to the police."

I turned my back on him to walk out.

He tsk-tsked, and I hesitated, then turned to look at him again.

"My dear, do you really think a successful businessman of my stature would be so careless as to not acquire friends in the local police department?" He lifted one eyebrow, smiling all the while.

I froze in his doorway. Had he bought off the Chicago police?

His mocking laughter rang out again. "You can't prove anything anyway, so I think our little meeting is over. Run along now, I'm a busy man."

My shoulders stiff, I walked through his office door, down the stairs, and then fled out into the street.

CHAPTER 17

THE LAST STRAW

My eyes were hot with tears and I stumbled over my muddy hem as I ran down the sidewalk. Mr. Quigley was a monster, not a businessman, and he certainly was no gentleman. He'd plotted to take Papa's invention for his own from the very start. The sidewalk came to an end and I almost fell off of the curb into the street before I caught myself and made the turn to head around the side of the building. I gulped air and rubbed my knuckles over my eyes, trying to clear away the tears.

A violent rage was rising in me. Our house was all but lost, and there was nothing I could do about it.

And Henry. I was livid. How could I have been so wrong about him?

The realization that I'd spent three days racing after something that was already beyond my reach was staggering. Not only had I failed, I'd wasted time that would have been better spent at Papa's bedside. My stomach twisted with fear. I could never get that time back. I prayed that Papa still lived, and that I'd be home again in time to see him wake up.

I stomped along the gravelly path alongside the building, heading towards the alley. I was determined to confront Henry and be rid of him once and for all.

While I sometimes have difficulty understanding why people do the things they do, I'd never made such a terrible error in judgment about a person before. I'd been convinced Henry was trying to help me, when the whole time, we'd been at cross purposes. I saw his hand in every setback I'd suffered in my headlong race to Chicago. To say I was furious as I strode around the corner to face him was a vast understatement.

I would tell Henry Thorne exactly what I thought of him, and then without him I would head back to Cincinnati at top speed.

I stomped around the corner, and beheld a terrible sight.

The lovely magenta silk of the envelope hung loosely, split by many long gashes. The twin stovepipes were bashed in and bent over, and the door to the furnace had been kicked clear off its hinges.

Henry was nowhere in sight, but the man with the squinty eyes lay flat on his back unconscious on the ground next to the hull.

How in the world had this new disaster come to pass? I had only been inside a short while.

As my fury rose still higher, a roaring filled my ears.

The sound of running feet penetrated my thoughts over the roaring sound, and I turned to see who was coming up behind me.

"Theo!"

Henry pelted towards me down the sidewalk.

Out of breath, he skidded to a stop in front of me.

"I tried to stop him, but he'd already cut the envelope."

I clenched my fist tight and punched Henry in the eye with all of my strength. He fell to the ground, clutching his face.

"Ow! Why the devil did you do that?"

"Did you think your employer would keep your secret now that he no longer has any use for you?" I would have liked to have kicked him, but Papa always says you shouldn't kick a man when he's down. I strongly considered it though.

Henry blinked up at me. "That was only at first. I'm not working for him anymore, not since that night. Goshamighty, Theo, you pack a wallop."

I kicked dirt onto him, leaving him sputtering.

"You have schemed and lied," I fumed. "You are the worst swindler who ever lived."

"I didn't, I swear it!" He scrambled to his feet. "I've been true to you since I realized how things really were. Didn't I jump out to save you from crashing? Didn't I help rebuild her at your uncle's? They hung me from my ankles!"

"And now you've slashed her to pieces."

He pointed at the man lying to the side of the Kestrel.

"He did it, not me. When you didn't come back out, I headed toward Quigley's building to make sure you were okay. When I got to the corner, I heard the sound of him breaking the stovepipes, and I ran back to stop him."

"I don't believe you one bit."

"But I did." He spread his hands at his sides. "I saved you when they tried to shoot you!"

He pointed at the side of his head.

I folded my arms.

"Theo, please, you have to believe me. I'm trying to help you."

"Nothing you can say—no lie you can tell—can change my mind. Leave now, or—or I'll strike you again." I clenched both fists and raised them in front of me, ready.

"While you were in there I hired a wagon to load her onto so we can get to the train station. We have to hurry—"

"Stop. I don't want to hear it." I took a menacing step towards him.

"You have every reason to hate me, but I know this isn't what you're really like, please stop and listen."

I glared at him, and my words failed me.

"You're kind and compassionate." He gestured with his hands, speaking earnestly. "You could have let me fall and die in Richmond, but you didn't, even when it meant they got away again."

"That, sir, is the difference between me and you. I value life, even the worthless life of a thief. You only value what you can steal from some poor person."

Henry slowly backed away. "I—it's not like you think."

"Get away from me!"

He started to say something else, but seeing my mind was made up, instead he turned and ran down the street. I did not care where he went, as long as it was permanently out of my sight.

The man on the ground didn't move, so I sat down on the edge of the hull, stunned.

What had just happened? Had Henry slashed and kicked at my aetherigible in hopes I would cling to him or look to him for help—even when he had to have known I'd discover his betrayal with that odious man inside the building?

It seemed the greatest injustice that the betrayal came from the one person on whom my heart had attached itself. We had been playing the same game, but with different objectives. That he had trifled with me as part of his plan—well, that part was awful.

I shook myself mentally.

It would not do to dwell on what had happened. I looked up at the envelope and the broken metal. The Kestrel was ruined and would not fly. Now how would I get home?

As if in answer to my thought, a large cargo wagon pulled by two giant draft horses rumbled up. The two men clambered out, and placed a ramp so they could pull the Kestrel aboard.

I stood up and glared at them.

"What do you think you're doing?"

One of the men touched his cap. "Loading up, miss. We were hired to take her to the train station. To ship as freight."

My brows knit together. I didn't want anything to do with something *he'd* planned.

"I haven't any money to pay you, so you might as well stop."

"It's already paid for by the young man, miss. Tip and all."

That changed my mind. Even if Henry's dirty money had paid for it, I didn't see any reason to reject the ride and stay in Chicago. Another girl might have dissolved in tears at this latest interference from the one who had been so callous with her affections. But I steeled myself and decided to focus on getting home. If it resulted in less cash in Henry's pocket, so much the better.

I jerked the silk off of the frame.

"Here, let me get that, miss." The man gently folded the envelope and placed it into the hull while the other man disassembled the frame. Everything stowed, they resumed loading the Kestrel. The horses stood patiently as the two men heaved and pulled, sliding her up the ramp and into the wagon bed.

Sweat dripped from the man's brow, and he wiped it with a red kerchief as he made his way back over to me. He stood for a moment, gazing down at the unconscious form of Squinteye.

"What about this one here? Is he your man?" He pointed to Squinteye.

"Heavens no, he's no concern of mine. Leave him here to sleep it off."

"Very well, miss. Will you be coming along with your freight? It's no fancy passenger carriage, but there's room for you up on the seat."

"Yes, I think I will. Thank you." I took his proffered hand and climbed aboard.

The trip to the train station only took a short time.

The tracks bustled with activity for a Thursday. In spite of the scene I'd just been through, the ride had calmed me and five strong men struggling to hoist a large circular contraption up into the boxcar caught my eye. The name burned onto the wooden packing stand read Hot Vapor Uniwheel. A seat on a sliding piece inside the wheel was arranged behind a steering yoke, along with a tiny but powerful looking engine that I could only surmise was a new means of personal transportation.

Daydreaming about other people's inventions would do me no good, so I snapped myself out of my reverie and climbed down. I caught the foreman's attention and once they finished moving the uniwheel to one side of the door, he directed the men to lift the Kestrel out of the bed of the wagon.

After three days of hard use, my poor little craft looked awful. She was scraped and scratched from stem to stern. I stood nervously by to see to it that she was safely loaded, but I had to face facts, there wasn't much left intact that could still be damaged on her. With her safely aboard, I squared my shoulders and headed over to the ticket window try to talk my way aboard the train without any money.

The line moved quickly, and soon I was at the window. I drew breath to begin pleading my case but the agent spoke first.

"Miss Theodocia Hews? Your fare's already been paid." He pushed a ticket across the counter.

"How could you know my name? How did—who?" I sputtered.

"The ticket was paid for by the same gentleman who paid the freight charge. Platform five."

"That was no gentleman," I growled. Irritated, I snatched up the ticket.

I needed to get back to Cincinnati, but I sincerely hoped Henry was not planning to take the same train as I was. I couldn't stand the thought of him near me.

The third regular fare passenger car was nearly empty, and I found a seat in the back next to a window. I pushed it open and let the lake breeze flow in over me to cool my face. Placing my goggles and handkerchief on the seat next to me to deter anyone from sitting there, I rested my head against the tall seatback and closed my eyes to wait. If he did board, I would pretend to be asleep.

Time passed. There seemed to be some delay. I tilted my head out the window to see railroad men clustered around a piston on the car ahead.

I leaned my head back once more and dozed.

With a loud whistle and a sharp jerk, the train began to leave the station. There were still but a few passengers in the car, and no sight of Henry. The train moved slowly at first, creaking and rocking over the many crossings on its way out of town. After a while, looking out my window, I noticed the townhouses giving way to woods and fields, and I felt the train pick up speed.

I took a deep breath, and let it out slowly. The car held only four other people. Henry was not here.

All of the emotions I had held in check began swirling through my head. My worry for Papa, my horror that I'd done the wrong thing in chasing after the twins, the taunts from that horrible Mr. Quigley, my terrible decision to let myself fall for Henry. The tears began again, and this time I could not stop them. I tried to be unobtrusive, but I fear my sniffling was noticeable.

An older woman traveling alone left her seat in the middle of the car and swayed down the aisle toward me. "Are you all right, my dear?" she asked kindly.

"I will be, once I get back home."

She patted my arm with one slender gloved hand. "Ah, the big city can be so hard on young hearts. There, there."

I didn't bother to correct her. She offered me her lavender scented hanky, and I gratefully took it. I blew my nose and smiled weakly, and she patted me again and returned to her seat.

I wiped my eyes and sat back, trying to make myself comfortable in the firm upholstered seat.

The metal wheels hummed on the rails, the car swayed from one side to the other rhythmically, and the cool breeze rushed past my face. Exhausted in mind and body, I listened to the rails sing their siren song and slowly drifted away into sleep.

Clouds floated alongside my airship. A hand grasped my shoulder and shook me gently.

"Theo," a voice whispered gently in my ear in my dream.

As I glided along through the skies of my dream, I could practically feel the warmth of the fingers through my jacket as the shaking began again, this time more urgently.

I sighed and slowly opened my eyes.

Henry crouched in the aisle next to me gazing up into my face, his right eye already blackening. I jerked back out of his reach and banged my head against the window.

My brows drew together. "Why won't you let me be? Haven't you done enough damage already?"

"You have to listen to me. Mr. Quigley is on this train. He's taking the vocalizer with him to New York, and we have one more chance to get it back."

I scowled at him. "You are lying again. Mr. Quigley said he'd already sent it on, and anyway this train is going to Cincy."

He shook his head, then reached forward and drew the ticket out of my front pocket and silently handed it to me. It said Chicago Nonstop Express to New York. My stomach clenched into a hard knot. I didn't have time to go to New York, I had to get home.

"What have you done?" My eyes and face accused him, and I saw him flinch.

"It was the only way. I'd already hired the men to haul your airship when you came out of Quigley's office. Now you have to listen to me. Mr. Quigley and his man have gone into the dining car. They don't have anything with them, so the vocalizer must be in his private compartment in the first class car."

I eyed him disdainfully. I didn't want to listen. I didn't want to have anything to do with him at all. "Why are you telling me this?"

"I tried to tell you before but it just seemed easier to get you on the train. I've been watching the dining car, and now is our chance." He put his hand on the seat next to me. I eyed it like it was a snake.

His voice was quiet, so quiet I had to strain to make out what he was saying over the sound of the train. "What I did was wrong. Even though he paid me ten dollars, I never should have climbed up on your roof. I tried to say this to you before. You have every right to hate me, but please let me try to make it right."

I sat for a moment, thinking frantically. It was already Thursday afternoon. If I got my hands on the vocalizer, I would still have until tomorrow to get it to Papa's buyer. I shook my head.

"Even assuming I'm able to break into his compartment, I'm stuck on this train with him. He'll just send Squinteye back to this car to take it back from me."

His eyes bored into mine. "Not if I uncouple the engine and first class car from the dining car and the rest of the train."

I considered what would happen if the train came uncoupled. If the engineer or his brakeman didn't immediately notice the engine was going faster without the weight of the other cars, the stokers in the tender surely would when they no longer had to shovel coal at such a high rate.

"Your plan is no good. The engineer will know right away. He'll just stop and reverse to recouple."

Henry's face split in the crooked, dangerous smile that I liked so much.

"Not if he thinks the dining car is on fire, he won't. I'll just jump off when it slows down and set a fire outside as a diversion. You'll tell him the dining car is on fire, and the engineer will see the smoke and go on to Toledo to get help. You can catch another train there and still arrive in Cincy on Friday," he said.

"You're crazy."

"Maybe so, but this is our chance. Do you want that vocalizer or not?"

"I can't believe I'm even considering trusting you. Is this some fresh trick of Mr. Quigley's?"

"The only thing I did for Mr. Quigley was to untie the Kestrel from your roof." He looked at me intently. "I swear it. I've been on your side ever since then, no matter what he said. Now we don't have much time. Will you let me help you?"

CHAPTER 18

WHERE THERE IS SMOKE

In the end, I didn't have a choice. I was on the wrong train, and if I wanted to go home today, my only chance was to do as he said and try to get the train to stop at Toledo. So I held back the ugly words I wanted to say, and instead, I nodded and followed Henry.

When we reached the forward second class car, he stopped me at the door and stripped off his coat to put on a white porter's jacket and a cap he'd held tucked under his arm. He tied on a long white apron and pointed to a laundry bin on wheels.

I grasped it by the handle. "What exactly do you want me to do with this? No one could possibly mistake me for a porter."

"I have to get you past the dining car somehow. You're not going to push it. Get in."

"Won't he recognize you?"

"I'll pull the cap down low over my eyes so Quigley doesn't notice me. Besides, the twins were the ones who hired me, so he shouldn't even know who I am."

The laundry bin had dirty linens in it, and I wrinkled my nose. "Won't all the first class sleeper compartments already be made up?"

"I'm sorry, but this is the best I could come up with, unless you'd rather climb up on top of the roof and jump from car to car."

He lifted up an armful of linens and glanced over his shoulder to make certain no one was watching. After I'd given him a long hard glare, I reluctantly climbed in and hunched down in the bottom. He piled the linens on top of me and my breathing quickly became stuffy and uncomfortable.

"Now be still," he hissed, and the wheels of the bin began to move.

The roar of the train told me when we passed through the doors and moving floor plates between the cars. Without anyone stopping us or speaking to Henry, we wheeled through the smoking car, then the kitchen car, and I froze because I knew the dining car and Mr. Quigley came next.

The roar of the train and the open air told me we were between cars, then the door squeaked open, and we were inside the dining car. I could hear the small clinks of cutlery on china and the voices of the first class passengers as they conversed as they supped. Henry paused then excused himself once when he was in someone's way, and we rolled forward.

Then I heard two distinctly foreign voices talking and laughing and my stomach took a loop. Henry had said the twins weren't in the dining car.

I trembled in fear they would recognize Henry. There was a slight pause, and I thought we were caught, but then Henry murmured something and the bin rolled on. The voices were behind us. I heard the next door between the cars open up, there was the loud sound of the train and the air rushing past again, and then we were into the first class car.

"Stay put," Henry hissed. I heard a doorknob rattle, and then another one. Finally, a door squeaked open. The bin lurched sideways, and I heard the door close. The pile of cloth lifted up off of me.

"We're in luck," Henry said, "this compartment was empty."

I straightened up. Ignoring his offer of a hand, I climbed out on my own.

"Now what?"

"We don't have much time. You'll have to break into his compartment—it's Number Eight, and find the vocalizer, then I'll pull the pin to separate the cars."

It seemed straightforward enough, but I didn't like it. "What if Mr. Quigley or the twins see you?"

"I'll make some sort of diversion in the dining car if anyone's watching me."

"Was Squinteye there with them?"

"I didn't see him, but his meal was still on the table. He must have gone to the necessary room."

"What if he comes back to this car to check on the vocalizer?"

"I won't let him. As soon as you get it, just lock yourself into this compartment."

"I don't have a key to use to get in to take it."

"Here." Henry handed me a filed down key.

I frowned at the reminder of his criminal trade, but I took it.

"This key should work on all the doors in the train," he said.

"The twins have pistols," I reminded him.

"Let me worry about that. Now hurry."

He pushed the bin out into the passage and back the way we'd come. I made my way to the middle of the car. Through sheer nerves, I nearly started opening the lock on Number Six before I saw my error and moved to the right door.

I saw no one in the corridor. I fervently hoped all the first class passengers had left their compartments for the dining car. I knelt down and slipped the key into the lock. I wiggled and tickled the tumblers with the key, but it didn't open. I was in continual anxiety as to whether someone would come out of a door, or that a porter or the conductor would come into the car. Finally, with a tiny metallic *snick*, the lock gave and the door fell open.

Squinteye stood beside the bunk, pointing a gun straight at me. One eye was blackening and a red welt lay across his forehead. This time, he wasn't smiling.

He rushed through the door and roughly grabbed my upper arm. "You again. Come with me." He thrust the gun into his waistband and shoved me along the passage ahead of him and into the dining car.

There stood Mr. Quigley, lounging against the edge of a dining table, a cigar stub in his mouth. The twins, seated on either side of him, turned at the exact same time to see me. They sneered to each other.

Henry hadn't been on the connector between the cars, and he was nowhere to be seen now that I was in the dining car. My stomach gave a lurch. Had he planned this all along?

Being afraid wasn't going to do me any good. I straightened my shoulders and held my head high. Among my friends and family, I must confess, I am not known for my outward quietness in the best of situations. I coolly contemplated the three of them for a moment, but I could not hold my tongue.

"Hell is empty and all the devils are here."

"A true lady does not curse, mademoiselle," said one of the twins. Her sister laughed, a nasty nasal sound.

"I am not cursing, you stupid French trollop, I am quoting Shakespeare."

"Enough. What is this, Harvey?" said Mr. Quigley.

"I caught her trying to break into your compartment," Squinteye said.

Mr. Quigley blew a puff of foul smoke into my face and took his seat.

"The trouble with you, my dear, is that you don't seem to know when to quit."

I gritted my teeth and glared at him. I would *not* rise to the bait.

"Perhaps she would like to view the scenery from ze platform between ze cars?" said Fleura to Quigley under her breath.

Or maybe it was Angelique. I could not tell them apart, nor did I care.

"That's an idea," said Quigley.

I looked around the dining car in desperation. A few of the other tables were occupied by first class diners, but most were eating their food or talking to one another, and none of them were paying the slightest bit of attention to me. None of the dining car attendants nor any of the porters were there. Were all these people in league with Mr. Quigley? I didn't know who I could turn to for help.

Squinteye shoved me roughly toward the door. Two men a table away looked up in surprise as I stumbled and grasped the edge of their table.

"Easy there," said Squinteye, and he grasped my arm again and moved me toward the door.

"I—aagh." He gripped my arm so painfully I gasped.

"Bumpy ride. Excuse us." He tipped his hat to the men, who returned to their conversation.

The laundry bin was shoved up against the wall beside the last table. As we reached the end of the aisle, I drew breath to scream, but Squinteye clapped his hand over my mouth. I grabbed at the door jamb in panic. How could it be that no one noticed him manhandling me?

I heard a loud crash as the laundry cart overturned, knocking into a table and upsetting the cut glass lamp burning there. Henry crawled out from the linens.

People leaped up from their tables in surprise as Quigley stood and drew a pistol. Henry stood still, looking back and forth between me, Squinteye, and Quigley. The laundry cart burst into flames.

Cries and screams broke out as all the other passengers began shoving toward the back of the train to escape the chaos. The twins ran with them.

Henry took a step away from the flames and towards Quigley, who lowered his gun. What was Henry doing? I wrenched free from Squinteye and pushed forward through the door into the rushing wind of the platform. I shoved the door closed, but the ugly man's arm was already through and he flung the door open, knocking me to the metal platform between the cars, which was shifting and pinching together then apart under my hands.

He grimaced menacingly and grabbed my ankle. I clung to the railing and kicked with all my might, catching him in the arm and sending his gun flying away into the shrubs flashing past.

He snarled and grabbed at me again, but got only a fistful of skirt hem. I kicked wildly, catching a glancing blow on his chin. He swung his bot savagely at my feet and my legs flew sideways under the railing into the open air, perilously close to the gap between the rails.

The wind whipped my skirts and I clutched the middle bars with both arms. I struggled to get my legs back onto the platform, but my skirt had tangled in the mechanism that linked the cars. I let go with one hand and yanked desperately at them. Squinteye seized two handfuls of my skirt and tore it away. Without much in the way of petticoats, the skirt of my dress ripped easily, leaving only a short portion of fabric covering my waist and upper thighs, freeing me from the linking pin. The key Henry had given my dropped out of my pocket as I struggled, clinking as it bounced off the metal plate. Only my arms and hands on the rail were holding me in place on the jiggling platform.

Squinteye grabbed one of my wrists and began wrenching my fingers away from the rail. I wrapped the other arm back around, but he kept loosening my grip. He plainly meant to throw me from the train.

Squinteye swung and punched me viciously in the face. I saw stars, but somehow managed to keep clinging to the rail, my fingers tingling strangely. With each lurch of the train, Squinteye swayed precariously toward the opening in the rail between the two cars.

I drew my legs up. The train violently pitched left and then right, throwing him against the other side. With all my might, I gripped the rail and kicked out with both feet. My feet tingled with the impact. At that very moment, the train jolted over another big bump with a clang of metal plates. Squinteye scrabbled for a grip but his hands clutched only air, and he fell backwards through the gap in the railing, disappearing from sight as the train rushed on. A huge blue spark crackled on the railing near where he'd last stood, startling me. It must have been a discharge of static electricity built up from the passage of the train over the tracks.

Breathing in great gasps, I clung to the rail for a moment. When the quivering weakness left my arms, I wriggled under the rail and back onto the platform. By now, dark smoke trailed back from the dining car. There was no sign of Henry. Had he betrayed me again and left me to fend for myself against these villains?

I didn't know. But his plan was still sound. I heaved up the heavy metal plate and looked at the linking mechanism for a moment, trying dizzily to ignore the sight of the massive railroad ties flashing past below. I reached down and grasped the pin, but try through I might, it wouldn't budge.

Well if I couldn't separate the cars, I could still go get the vocalizer and climb out the front of the private car to signal the engineer and tenders. I wrenched open the door handle of the private car.

A shot rang out from somewhere within the smoky dining car behind me and shattered the glass window in the door I held in my hands, pelting me with shards. The gun went off again, and I jumped into the private car and ducked down just inside the half-open door, peeking through the broken window, frantic to know what had happened.

Thick black smoke billowed out of the windows on both sides of the dining car, blown backwards by the speed of the train. I couldn't see anyone inside the car for the smoke.

What was happening?

The door opened and Henry emerged, coughing. A great wave of relief washed over me.

"I like that dress," he rasped, smiling at me.

I rolled my eyes.

"Go inside and lock the door." He pointed to the first class car.

I took one step inside, but then I stayed where I was. He heaved up the plate and lay down on his stomach to reach for the pin below. He grasped it with one hand, but it would not move.

He got onto his feet again and squatted down to pull with both hands.

The remaining glass in the door behind him blew out, and something smacked into the wood of the door frame beside my face, making me flinch.

Henry jerked his head up and his eyes met mine, but he kept both hands on the pin. "Get inside," he yelled.

The door behind him burst open and the smoke cleared to reveal Quigley doubled over and coughing violently, his face covered in streaks of soot and his gun still clutched in one hand.

Seeing the fear in my eyes, Henry darted a quick look back over his shoulder. He gave a great heave, but the pin still held.

Quigley hacked and spat. He clutched the door frame and dragged his sleeve across his streaming eyes, trying to see.

"What the devil are you doing, Thorne? You said you'd go get her! Where's Knez?"

Henry ignored what Quigley was saying and kept working at pulling the pin.

Quigley had to grip the door frame to keep his balance as he blinked and coughed some more. His eyes met mine. He frowned and tried to give Henry a shove with his foot. "Can't you hear me, boy? Remember who pays your salary. Stop that and grab her." He raised the gun unsteadily, trying to point it at me, but was overcome with another bout of coughing.

I felt a moment of doubt, but without so much as a glance at Quigley behind him, Henry gathered himself for one more effort, and this time he put his back into it and pulled mightily.

"Stop that right now!" growled Quigley, lowering the gun toward Henry's head.

The pin popped out and Henry crashed backwards, knocking Quigley back inside the car. I heard Quigley curse, and then I heard the sharp report of the pistol.

"Henry!" My shrill cry blew away with the wind.

Henry slowly sagged to the bottom of the dining car doorway, and the cars began to separate. A pair of hands reached for Henry and dragged him into the smoky interior.

Freed from the great weight of the long train, the locomotive and the first class car in which I stood raced on—farther and farther away from the fiery dining car and the rest of the train. And Henry.

CHAPTER 19

ON THE HORNS OF A DILEMMA

After I spent several unsuccessful minutes trying to pick the lock of Quigley's compartment with a hairpin, I finally broke the door by bashing the flimsy frame with my shoulder—which hurt like the dickens. I hopped around the passageway shouting several unladylike words, hoping that all of the first class passengers had felt hungry enough to go to dinner before the fire.

I had to ransack the place to find my father's invention, and that was as odious an undertaking as you could imagine, as the unpleasantly strong scent of Quigley's hair oil seemed to cling to his every possession. Pawing through his things was a revolting thing for a lady to have to do, but I steeled myself and kept looking.

Finally, I found the vocalizer and the remote listening device, both wrapped carefully in cotton batting and hidden within a scratched black leather satchel inside one of Quigley's larger pieces of luggage. The vocalizer seemed safe enough, though I couldn't tell whether or not it still worked by its appearance and I had no time to test it.

After repacking the vocalizer, I made my way forward with the satchel through the deserted car and out onto the forward most deck. The car immediately in front of me was the large tender. Fully loaded when we'd left the station in Chicago, the coal bunker was still heaped so high that I could not see past the pile of gleaming black chunks.

The exposed pistons that ran the pumps which fed the water into the locomotive were moving at a furious pace to keep the boiler's pressure up, so I knew there must be a team of men up there in front of the coal, frantically shoveling.

Whistling, shouting, and screaming did no good at all, so finally I went back into Quigley's compartment and gathered up the three glass lamp chimneys and carried them forward. They were beautifully wrought of colored glass, thick and heavy to withstand the rigors of travel by train. One at a time, I threw them over the coal pile. After a particularly well aimed third try landed just about where I estimated the men were shoveling, the angry face of the fireman popped up to glare at me over the pile of coal.

I did my best to use hand signals to communicate to him about the missing train. His furrowed eyebrows and straining neck veins quickly passed to a vexed variety of confusion. Another face appeared beside his—one of the stokers no doubt—and the fireman directed this second man to climb to the top of the water jacket to take a better look. I could see them gesturing back and forth until the second man finally climbed back down and shouted directly into the fireman's ear, then both faces disappeared. In the next moment I had to grab onto the railing as the brakes of the great locomotive began shrieking.

The train slowed to three-quarter speed, and a succession of faces climbed up to look back over the tender and the roof of the first class car no doubt to confirm that the rest of the train was missing.

We had nearly hurtled past Delta, Ohio before I'd caught the attention of the fireman. Just as Henry had said, they couldn't very well reverse down the tracks to recouple the burning car, so we continued on to Toledo. Once there, the engineer stopped her in the station, the men climbed down, and a flurry of activity began besides the tracks.

The engineer stood cursing the fireman for not realizing that the train had suddenly become many thousands of pounds lighter. The fireman stood, arms crossed tightly in front of his chest, steadfastly insisting the latest improvements to the boiler and engine had resulted in greater speed with less coal shoveled. His three stokers stood mutely behind him, looking uncomfortable.

I climbed down from the car and strode over to them, the leather satchel held firmly in my right hand. The eyes of all five men swung down to fix on my ankles, and as a cooling breeze touched my knees, I abruptly remembered that most of my skirt was missing.

"If only I had Mr. Goff's pants, I wouldn't be in this impossible situation," I muttered to myself. Trying to ignore their flabbergasted faces, I quickly related what had happened to the train.

I'm not sure which astonished them more, my story or my indecent appearance, but it hardly matter because by then the station manager and several other representatives of the railway line had swarmed the platform having heard the news from the water stop north of the little town of Montpelier.

One blushing young man—a ticket agent I thought—carried a white linen tablecloth to me, and I gratefully wrapped myself up. He guided me through the station past a group of scandalized travelers, then into an office where he silently pulled out a chair and held it for me, and then proceeded to make me a pot of tea. The brew was strong and I lifted the cup to breathe in its soothing fragrance. Out of the corner of my eye, I spotted the young man tiptoeing out the door.

"Sir?"

He froze in place, his hand on the knob.

"You've been very kind, but would it be possible for you to go see to it that a doctor is sent to the stranded train? My friend—a dark haired young man—was shot right before my eyes as the cars separated." I couldn't help but worry about Henry.

I shifted in my seat, and the tablecloth unwound from my legs and slithered to the floor. "Bother," I said, snatching it back up.

His face turned even redder. "I believe it is standard company procedure to send a full complement of doctors and policemen to any wreck, but I'll go inquire." He averted his eyes and tried to back his way out of the door again.

"Sir?"

He raised his eyes and kept them glued rigidly on mine. "Yes, miss?"

I pulled the tablecloth back up. "I will need a ticket on the next train to Cincinnati. Could I impose upon you to make the arrangements?"

He cleared his throat delicately. "Are you sure you wouldn't prefer to continue on to New York?"

I arched one eyebrow at him. "I was tricked onto the Express by the men responsible for the wreck. I wish to go to Cincinnati. Is that a problem?"

"Of course not. The company is sorry for the inconvenience. I'll see to it at once." He bowed and stepped backwards.

"One more thing..."

He straightened up and brought his eyes up to mine, his hopes of escaping dashed yet again. "Yes, miss?"

"If you happen to have any abandoned luggage lying about the station, I would be grateful if you could bring it to me. I am in need of decent clothing." I raised the corner of the tablecloth and gestured at my leg. He went pale.

"At once, miss." He hurried out, closing the door firmly behind him.

I sighed and sat back in my chair, casting my eyes around the manager's office where the assistant had put me. The window in one wall allowed the manager to see the ticket counter so he could keep an eye on things. Right now, there was a bustle of activity as four agents worked furiously to check passenger lists and schedules in an effort to be ready for the influx of angry passengers from the interrupted express. I wondered why I didn't warrant the attention of the station manager himself. Had he gone with the police, firemen, and doctors down the tracks to the burned car and engineless train?

The assistant came back in and wordlessly dropped two embroidered satchels and a large ornate tooled leather bag. I rifled through them right away. The leather bag was filled with expensive dresses meant for a much larger woman, but one of the satchels had a gray dress close enough to my size that I thought I could wear it. I quickly unbuttoned my ruined travel dress to change with hardly a thought for the original owner. Desperate times called for desperate measures. I slipped my jacket back on over the new dress.

Now clad more decently, I clutched the vocalizer satchel to me and opened the door to venture out into the passenger area of the station to find the ladies washroom. I splashed some water on my face, dried it on a hand towel, and endeavored to repair my windblown hair as best I could without a comb or brush. Finished, I checked out my image in the mirror. The dress didn't look half bad.

The clock in the station said half past two. If I had any hope of getting back to Cincinnati by evening, I'd have to board a train immediately. Before I could begin worrying, the assistant came up to me, waving a ticket in his hand.

"This is for the next train to Cincinnati. It has stops in Columbus and Xenia, but it's the most direct fare I could get for you."

I took the ticket from his hand. "Thank you. When does it leave?"

He pulled out his heavy, gold pocket watch and flicked it open. "The train will leave at twenty past three, on the dot. Boarding should begin in thirty minutes, Platform C."

"Thank you. I should like to mention what a good job you've done to your manager. Is he nearby?"

"Over there. He's speaking to the policemen that just came in."

A cluster of railroad workers, agents, the station manager, and a couple of members of the local police had gathered at the ticket counter. I threaded my way into the circle. A tall, younger policeman was speaking in excited tones.

"...dining car was entirely burned out, all the way down to the iron wheels. The passengers pulled out the last two people inside before the flames filled the car—two men—and the younger one was to blame for everything."

My heart caught in my throat. To blame for everything? "Was he all right?" I blurted out.

All eyes turned to me.

The young policeman shook his head. "He's shot through the shoulder by the gentleman who stopped him from burning all the cars up—some important businessman from Chicago—but the young scoundrel is right enough to stand trial for what he did."

"But it wasn't his fault," I sputtered. "He did the things he did because of Quigley—the businessman. He's the real villain."

The policeman rubbed the end of his nose with his finger. "That's not how I heard it. How would you know anyway? No disrespect intended, miss."

"I was there on the train when it happened! I told the whole story to the engineer. Haven't the police taken his statement?"

He shook his head. "The engineer and his men are trying to help clear the burnt hulk off of the tracks to hook the rest of the train back up so's he can haul it into the station to get a new dining car and fuel up again. If you have a statement to make, you'd best come with me to the station."

My stomach sunk. I could hardly process what I had heard. Henry had been shot, but he was alive, and apparently so was Quigley, who had laid the blame for the whole incident on Henry's head. Naturally the police believed the false story from the smooth-talking businessman over the word of the young thief.

I turned to the station manager. "Sir? Surely you can go and straighten this out. The young man, Henry Thorne, is not to blame. He was forced to act as he did by Quigley."

The manager looked from me to the policeman. "I can't possibly leave now. All of those passengers will need to be re-ticketed."

"Statements need to come from eyewitnesses, miss," said the policeman.

I checked the large clock on the wall. The time was just after half past two. Forty-nine minutes until my train pulled out from Platform C.

My mind froze.

For three days, I had been trying my darndest to get the vocalizer back to Cincinnati in time to hand it over to Papa's buyer. Now I had it safely in my hands, and all I had to do was jump aboard the train to take me to Mr. Tamm's office. And then I could go on to our house, where I could see if Papa was awake again. Why was I hesitating?

"What will happen to him? The young man, I mean."

The young policeman put his hand on the handcuffs on his belt and jingled them. "Into a jail cell."

"The Chicago New York Express Railway Company will prosecute the culprit to the fullest extent of the law," said the station manager, raising his chin.

"But I've just said he isn't guilty. There's far more to this than Quigley is letting on." I clenched my fingers around the handle of the satchel. Why weren't they listening to me?

The screech of locomotive brakes told me a train had arrived, and I could tell at a glance from the billows of steam the location was Platform C. Ordinary passengers began stepping out of the cars and moving through the station.

Thoughts whirled through my brain. Henry was a thief, that much was true. He should have to pay for his crimes, shouldn't he? But Mr. Quigley was the real brains behind everything that had happened. It would be a miscarriage of justice if he blamed Henry for everything and simply walked away from all the harm he'd done unscathed. No mention had been made of the twins either. They were likely still at large.

Henry had done his best to create a distraction in the dining car out of loyalty to me, in hopes of making things right between us by allowing me to get the vocalizer back. Surely he hadn't meant to catch it on fire? It wouldn't be right to let him face real jail time for something he didn't do.

The men stood there looking at me.

I grasped at the arm of a ticket agent. "Sir? Are there any more trains to Cincinnati today?"

"Not until much later, and it's the overnight freight train. No passengers."

People were scurrying around on Platform C. Porters were assisting passengers with luggage, moving toward the cars.

Why was I lingering, unable to decide? I didn't have time for the police. I had to get back to Papa. I had been gone since Tuesday night. Who knew what his condition was now? What if he'd been calling for me? What if he'd…?

I couldn't finish that thought. Papa had to be all right. Dr. Jepson would see to it.

The handle of Quigley's satchel weighed heavily in my right hand. I had to finish what I'd set out to do, our very livelihood depended upon my delivering the vocalizer on time. I hoped Papa had left Mr. Tamm's address on his desk.

I shook my head and tried to gather my scattered thoughts.

I didn't owe Henry anything, even if I had kissed him. After all, he had intended us harm when he'd abruptly appeared in my life.

My fingernails dug into the handle, scoring the worn leather. Why wouldn't my feet move?

Another young police officer rushed up. "They've got him on the handcar, and they're rushing him here. I've got the wagon ready outside to take him straight to the station."

The first policeman motioned me forward. "Come on, miss, I'll need you to come with me if you're going to make a statement."

I frowned. "But he was shot. Shouldn't you take him to the hospital?"

The second police officer looked quizzically at me, his brows knit together. "This is police business, miss, if you won't come make a statement, we'll be leaving." He and the other officer began walking away. The railroad employees all went back to their work, leaving me standing there alone.

Platform C was crowded as the passengers checked their watches and waited for the doors to open. The Conductor was making a pass alongside the train, examining the folding stairs and doors. The time to board had not yet come.

Still, my feet were frozen to the floor.

"Theodocia," I muttered to myself, "you have to get on that train."

The two police officers reached the end of the station and one pushed open the door to the street. They paused there in the doorway, talking about something or another.

A surge of pressure filled my chest and rose up into my throat until I felt like I could no longer breathe. The ticket agents had all wandered back to their counter. No one was paying the least bit of attention to me.

What would Papa want me to do? Henry had been falsely accused. The injustice of it all was ghastly, and I couldn't get past that.

I thought about the times I had been blamed for things that I hadn't done. Even though I've done a lot of things in my life that might skim along the wrong side of the rules, I'd always had a highly developed sense of what was right and what was wrong. Papa had raised me to stand up for those who could not help themselves. Yet I also owed a duty to my father. If I acted now, it would affect him and possibly spoil our lives.

I stood alone in the middle of the floor, paralyzed. I took a great gulp of air, and held it. A calmness came over me, and then something inside me burst free. I could not let Henry go to jail for something he hadn't done.

"Wait!"

The first police officer turned to look at me.

"I—I think I will make a statement! It won't take long, will it? I have forty-five minutes until my train leaves."

I dashed across the room to where the policemen stood waiting for me, and I followed them out through the door and on toward their horse and wagon.

CHAPTER 20

AN UNEXPECTED OUTCOME

The second police officer climbed up on the seat and took up the reins as I got to the side of the wagon. I reached up for the handle, but the other man stopped me.

"Oh no, miss, that wagon is for the prisoner. I'll walk you to the Police Station. It's not far."

"Be quick about it." I tried to push a rising sense of panic away.

We walked along the shady sidewalk, and in just four minutes as he'd promised, we reached the station. He opened the door and I walked into the hot and airless interior. An older officer with thick gray muttonchop whiskers looked up from his paperwork, then rose and came over to the counter.

"This young lady was on the train. She's a witness, and would like to make her statement."

The older man opened the half-door in the counter to let me in. "Right this way, miss."

I tried to put my thoughts in order. Where would I even begin?

He pulled out a chair, holding it for me, and once I was seated he pulled out a thick pad and licked the lead of his pencil. "Now then, what is your name and address?"

He patiently led me through a series of questions. Several times as I described the vocalizer or flying in my aetherigible, he raised an eyebrow, but he methodically took it all down. It didn't take long.

I had calmed to the point where I didn't sound like a crazy woman—however improbable my story might sound to him. I gave him the name of the police chief at home who had led the investigation after the attack on Papa. I gave dates, times, motives, and I gave him the address of Quigley's office, and a description of the twins. I told him how Dr. Jepson and I gave statements to our precinct police.

He seemed most interested in my account of how and where Squinteye had fallen from the train after attacking me.

"So you say you singlehandedly fought this man off? That he attacked you on the platform between cars?"

"Yes. That's about it. Now I need to go catch my train." I rose from my chair.

A clamor arose out front, and a group of officers hustled inside, two of them supporting Henry. His face was drawn and pale under the black streaks of soot, and they had wrapped a makeshift bandage around his shoulder, but it had bled through. He kept his eyes cast down on the floor in front of him as they escorted him to the holding cell, and he didn't even see me standing not twelve feet from him.

The policemen laid him onto the cot in the cell. He looked ghastly. He laid still, his eyes closed.

"Stay here a moment, miss," said the officer who'd been listening to me. Slowly, I sat back down. He crossed the room and in hushed tones, spoke to the Captain, who answered him animatedly. The officer nodded once or twice at what the Captain was saying, but all the while his eyes coolly examined me.

The Captain came over to the desk where I sat and picked up the papers, flipping through them. He looked at me again, sternly this time. "Young lady, these are serious charges you're making. Is this account accurate?"

I met his eyes and didn't waver. "Every word is true. Quigley is a blackguard who used his power and directed others to commit crimes to get him what he wanted."

"Whose pistol shot Mr. Thorne?"

"Mr. Quigley. I saw it with my own eyes as they fell back through the door of the dining car when Hen—Mr. Thorne pulled the pin."

"Well, that's a problem, because you see, Mr. Quigley's statement given at the wreck named a Mr. Harvey Knez as the triggerman who shot Mr. Thorne then leaped from the train."

"Impossible. Mr. Knez had already fallen off of the platform before the fire even started. You'll find him somewhere further back along the line."

"We're checking on that. So you say this entire incident has to do with Mr. Quigley trying to steal your father's invention?"

"Yes. It's very valuable. I think he either meant to sell it to someone or to produce it himself. I have it right here." I looked down at the satchel by my side.

"So Mr. Thorne's statement about Quigley's men blackmailing him in Cincinnati is true?"

This was news to me. I thought for a moment. I had to answer honestly, though I wasn't sure if it would help the situation or not. "I—I don't know anything about any blackmail. But it would certainly explain why he felt he had to do the things he did."

"I've sent word to the Cincinnati Central Police Station. They'll check it out."

The door swung open and a doctor came in. They led him straight to Henry.

I turned back to the Captain. "So what happens now? He'll go to the hospital, won't he?"

"We'll hold Mr. Thorne until our officers can check out his story and bring in Quigley, Knez, and the French sisters. Doc Feeney will fix him up."

As I watched, the doctor quickly took off the bandage, cut the sleeve off of Henry's shirt and roughly swabbed the wound in his shoulder. He pulled a roll of clean lint from his black leather bag and packed the wound then wrapped it quickly up again with clean linen. Henry didn't stir.

"Aren't you going to take out the bullet?" I asked.

The doctor never looked up from his work. "It went straight through. It should stop bleeding now that it's properly bound."

The captain stood holding the door to the cell open. "He needs to answer questions. How long until he wakes up?"

The doctor tied the bandage firmly and put away the roll, then drew forth a small vial, uncorking it. He smelling salts under Henry's nose a time or too, but still there was no movement.

"Hard to say. He lost some blood but his color is good, so I'd think he'll wake up before long." The doctor fastened his bag and stepped out through the cell door to leave. One of the younger men pushed it shut with a clang.

I was glad to see Henry was getting a little bit of medical care, but wasn't any more I could do to help him, so I stood and spoke to the older man who had taken down my story. "That's all I can tell you. It's time for me to head back to the station to board my train."

He exchanged glances with the Captain, who shook his head. "Not just yet," the older man said. "Come over here with me."

He led me over toward the cell where Henry lay and took up a large key to open the lock. He swung back the barred door, and took a hold of my arm. I thought perhaps he was giving me a chance to speak with Henry before I left.

I was wrong.

He took the satchel from my hand and forcefully guided me through the opening in the bars. The door swung shut with a clang.

"Wait! What the devil are you doing?"

"You might as well have a seat in there, miss."

The Captain walked over and gave me a measuring look.

"Why am I being held?" I sputtered.

"There are some major discrepancies between your statement and the one Mr. Quigley gave to me. He claims you're in league with the young man there. Until we get a chance to question the other passengers, you're a suspect in the train wreck. Plus there's the matter of that gadget you stole from the gentleman."

"No, this is quite impossible! Didn't you hear anything I said?"

He turned away from me and bent over his desk to examine something.

I grasped the bars, stomped my foot, and gave a little involuntary shriek, and I heard a couple of the other policemen laugh under their breath.

"Let me out! I have to catch the train! Captain!"

Without so much as glancing my way, the Captain turned his back on me and walked out the station's front door. Before it closed, I could hear the two quick blasts of a locomotive steam whistle. The train was leaving the station.

CHAPTER 21

SWALLOW MY PRIDE

The older policeman returned to his desk and put the satchel on the floor. All the while, he kept his gaze directed towards the papers there. He would not meet my eyes.

I'd made a terrible mistake. I sat down on the iron bench and cradled my face in my hands. How could I have been so stupid?

This was what came of consorting with known criminals. I'd tried to do the right thing, and what did I get in return for my pains? Those idiot policemen had locked me up. For all I knew, Henry had been paid by Quigley to take the blame for the wreck and to frame me so that I wouldn't be able to get away with the vocalizer. No doubt Quigley would be along any moment to collect his ill-gotten prize which now sat on the other side of the iron bars, out of my reach.

The two younger policemen left, and the station quieted. Officer muttonchops shuffled papers quietly on his desk, pausing now and then to write. The light from the late afternoon sun slanted in through the small window set high up in the wall of the cell, but I couldn't see anything outside except for the tops of a distant tree.

The large, official-looking clock on the wall kept tick-tick-ticking out the seconds.

"Theo?"

Over on the cot at the other side of the cell, Henry stirred and coughed. I didn't answer.

"Where are we?"

I folded my arms and looked at him crossly. "Jail. Thanks to you, I've missed the train home."

He pushed up on one elbow and winced. "How did I get here?"

"The police brought you down the tracks on a handcart."

He took in our surroundings and shrank down visibly. He raised a trembling hand to his forehead.

"I'm sorry," he said, "about all of it. Why didn't you get on a train to Cincinnati?"

"Because I couldn't stand to see you wrongfully accused." I fixed him with a look that was meant to wither him. "There's no sense talking about it. We only seem to go in circles."

Henry lay there, staring at his hand for a while, then he sighed quietly and closed his eyes.

I turned myself the other way on the bench so I wouldn't have to look at him. How had the past three days gone so wrong? It had been such a simple idea. Go get the vocalizer back. I'd expected it to take a day, two at the most.

If my father was awake, he must be worried half to death about me. Guilt stole through me, leaving me weak and shaky. I should have at least sent him a telegram from the Toledo Train Station to let him know where I was. Had Uncle Adolphus headed to Cincinnati after I left his farmhouse? I hadn't even thought to ask him to go check on my father. I'd been so sure I'd be back at Papa's bedside in no time at all. How could I have been so stupid? I sagged against the wall.

Another terrible thought struck me—what if they telegraphed the Mount Belvedere police and learned about the exploding gas lamps? They'd think I was a criminal too. I buried my face in my hands.

Tick.

Tick.

Tick.

The police station was silent except for the wretched clock on the wall. I would not let myself cry, but I couldn't think of any course of action but to wait.

And wait.

Hours passed. At some point in time, Henry coughed a few times then fell back into unconsciousness. Or maybe he was asleep. Tendrils of sympathy began to inveigle their way through me, and I felt the urge to walk across the cell to check on him, which only made me angrier at myself. The doctor had tended to Henry. I would not lift a finger. He could now go hang for all I cared.

More time passed.

I was thinking that I might go mad with all of the waiting when the door opened up and the Captain walked into the station. He was followed by the two other policemen who were escorting the twins.

They were squawking and squealing to each other in French, with an occasional "'Ow dare you!" or "Let me go!" thrown in for good measure. They kept pulling out of the grasp of the two officers and raising a ruckus fit to wake the dead. At least, they woke up Henry, so I was assuming they might be waking the dead next.

The officers had so much trouble they finally dragged the two of them over to the bars and looped one set of handcuffs through one bar to lock a bracelet onto each of them.

"Now sit down, and shut up!" shouted the Captain, shoving chairs at the two of them. He'd plainly had an earful bringing them in. He went over to the older policeman—who was still standing up behind his desk, his mouth hanging open in astonishment at the sight of the identical twins huffing and snorting their disapproval—and the two of them put their heads together and had a quick conversation. Then the one with the muttonchops hustled back out the door.

I was watching the Captain speak to the two younger officers and straining to hear what he was saying, when something hard hit me in the side of the head and landed in my lap. A black high heeled shoe with a bow fixed onto the low vamp toe.

I glared at little miss trollop.

"This is all your doing," she hissed. And her sister nodded, then put her nose high into the air.

"Oh, be quiet," I said. "You yourselves are to blame. You should be more careful in your choice of employment."

There was a flurry of fast, agitated French. I didn't understand any of it, but judging from their angry faces, they didn't like me very much.

"Give me back my slipper," the twin on the left said.

I picked up the shoe, glared straight into her eyes, and then deliberately dropped it bow-side down onto the dirty floor of the cell. Her sister restrained her as she let out a muffled a shriek of rage.

Henry had been silent this entire time, but with this latest outburst he managed to raise himself up to a sitting position. He sneaked a glance at me but quickly dropped his eyes when he saw I'd caught him looking. He gingerly touched his bandaged shoulder.

As the twins sputtered down into silence, I tried to resume listening to the conversation the Captain was having with the other two. The door flew open again and in marched officer muttonchops waving a folded piece of paper in his hand. He gave it to the Captain, and they all stood expectantly while he read it.

All four heads swiveled to look at me. I couldn't imagine why.

THE ROOFTOP INVENTOR

Muttonchops took the key to the cell off of the hook while the other two younger men took the cuffs off of the twins.

My heart began thumping in my chest.

"Captain? You aren't going to put them into the cell with us, are you?" I said.

The twins eyed me. They looked as though they'd like to get their hands on me. I stood up and shifted my weight from one foot to the other.

"Of course not. We've received a telegram from the Belvedere Precinct Chief."

"Mount Belvedere," I corrected.

He crossed the room and held the cell door open. "Chief Van der Pool and some others vouched for you. You're free to go."

Relief burst through my chest and my cheeks burned suddenly as I slipped through the cell door. "Thank you," I said meekly.

"I'm sorry you were delayed," he said.

I crossed over to where the satchel sat on the floor. "I'm taking this home to my father," I said. At last, I was going home.

The Captain held the door and leaned inside to look at Henry. "You too."

Henry's face was a wonder of open-mouthed surprise. "Me?"

"Yes, you. They want you to be a witness down in Cincy for the case against these two." He shrugged towards the twins, whose mouths had twisted into ugly scowls.

Henry stood and winced at the pain in his shoulder. He took a breath and held it, then straightened up and shuffled out of the cell, holding his arm very still as he moved.

I was just reaching for the handle of the front door to go outside when the obvious thought crossed my mind and I whirled around. "Wait. What about Mr. Quigley? Where is he?"

"We're looking for him. It seems he had the conductor and the firemen unload his racing steam carriage just after the wreck. He claimed he needed to check to be sure there wasn't any damage. In all the confusion, I'm afraid he got away."

My stomach sank. It must have shown on my face.

The Captain crossed over to open the front door for me. "Don't worry miss. We'll catch him. He has to stop for fuel and water all the time for that thing."

I turned toward Henry and we shared a look. I didn't think either of us would bet on them being able to catch that racing steam car.

The police Captain turned to face Henry. "You're expected at the Mount Belvedere Station in the morning. I'm releasing you on your own recognizance, but understand me young man, there will be a warrant for your arrest if you don't show up."

"Yes sir. I'll be there," Henry said.

"There's a freight train at the station right now switching cars. The engineer is a friend of mine. Now hurry up, they're expecting you."

"Thank you," I said.

Henry shook the man's hand as best he could, then we were outside in the warm evening air, walking along in awkward communal silence toward the station, me in front, him following after. The leather bag knocked against my leg with every other step.

Henry didn't say anything as he trailed after me, but his silence spoke volumes about his character. He was willing to put up with my anger instead of defending himself, because he held himself accountable for what had happened, that was plain.

I began to wonder if I'd been wrong to blame him. The whole mess was so complicated. He'd done bad things, but he had his reasons. And if I was being honest, I'd made the decision to try to free him from jail and missed that train all by myself. He hadn't induced me to do it through any words or actions. In fact, he'd tried to manage things so that I'd be able to speed back down to Cincinnati once I had the vocalizer. It just hadn't turned out the way he'd planned.

I pondered over what Julia would do were she in my position.

Unlike Julia, forgiveness isn't in my nature. I know I tend to harbor a grudge—to nurse it and tend it until it's a canker that won't go away. But maybe just this once, I needed to give forgiveness a try. I slowed my pace so that he could catch up.

"Henry, I...I was wrong to be angry at you. I'm sorry."

He shook his head. "No, I was the start of your troubles. I thought I could fix it, but I just kept getting you in deeper and deeper."

"Don't be silly. I decided to chase after the vocalizer before I even knew you were involved. Everything that's happened since, well, I need to take responsibility for it." I breathed in deeply, then let the air out. "I need to thank you for getting me onto that train, and my airship too, although—you could have been more open about what you were doing."

Henry laughed. "As I remember it, you were furious with me. I didn't think you would listen."

"I will neither admit nor deny that. I just hope my father has woken up while I've been gone. I miss him dreadfully."

Henry gazed steadily at me as we walked along. "I hope so too. And I'm going to see to it that Mr. Quigley and those other three get the punishment they deserve."

"If they can catch him."

We were approaching the train station now, and a large black engine huffed at the platform. The conductor waved urgently at us from where he stood alongside the train.

"If you're going to Cincinnati, you'll have to come this way to board the caboose," he said urgently as we reached him. With one hand, he motioned for us to hurry along. "This is a freight train, but we're making an exception under the circumstances."

I exchanged a glance with Henry.

The conductor led the way along the platform, walking briskly. "Your freight from the wreck is safely loaded in a box car." He handed me a claim ticket and opened the door of the caboose. "All aboard!" he said, and he put the whistle he wore on a lanyard around his neck up to his lips and blew. The engine answered with two sharp blasts of its own much louder steam whistle.

We sank gratefully onto the benches inside and with a series of powerful jerks, the train was under way.

CHAPTER 22

THE HOME STRETCH

As the big airship lines took over the skies the past ten years, the effect on rail travel has been fast and dramatic. Passenger trains—like the one I accidentally boarded out of Chicago—are a rarity nowadays, since most everyone prefers to fly where they want to go. And so that's how I found myself sitting on a hard bench inside a drafty caboose as the heavy, one-hundred-ten boxcar freight train made its slow and tedious way southward, making frequent stops for water and coal.

The jolting and jarring of the little red car in which we traveled was enough to make my teeth hurt, not to mention my backside. Before we'd gone very far, Henry stretched out on the floor and soon was sound asleep. I declare that man can sleep anywhere.

When the long, dark night had passed and morning broke, my muscles ached from a thousand repetitions of nodding asleep then catching myself before I fell off the bench and onto the dusty floor.

Finally, stop by inexorable stop, we drew closer to Cincy, and I began to recognize the landmarks outside of town. Saturday morning dawned bright and clear, and I was almost home.

The train's arrival in the station, the scramble to arrange for my aetherigible to be carted to the house, and my search for a driver to take me home all took place in a haze. Henry stood patiently by me the entire time until I managed to hail a carriage for hire, even though I'm sure he wanted desperately to go see to his grandmother.

Henry helped me climb up into the carriage and handed up the satchel. I was just about to thank him for all he'd done and say goodbye, when a policeman walked up and began speaking earnestly to him.

The carriage driver behind us shouted to move us along. When my driver turned to answer back over his shoulder, he saw me sitting down on the seat. Without so much as asking me, he slapped the reins on the horse's back and we drove off.

"Wait! I—" The carriage behind us surged forward to take our place by the curb.

I twisted around in my seat. "Goodbye, Henry."

He took a step in my direction and said something as we rolled away, but I couldn't hear what it was for all the noise from the busy street. All I could do was wave. It was not how I wanted to leave things with him, but I didn't try to stop the driver. I was headed home at last.

I was more tired than I'd ever been before, and in spite of myself I fell into a deep sleep as the driver headed towards the Seven Hills. So it seemed like only an instant had passed when the driver spoke to me, trying to wake me up.

I grabbed up the satchel and ran up the walk to the side door. I let myself in and sped up the back stairs to Papa's bedroom door.

The bed stood empty, neatly made up. My stomach gave a lurch.

"Emmoline? Are you downstairs?" My voice trembled. I walked back down the stairs, the satchel still in my hand.

"Theo?"

I froze in place two steps from the bottom.

"Theo? Is that you?"

I rushed through the house to the front parlor. There in a wingback chair drawn up close to the sunny window sat my father, a wool throw spread over his lap, awake once again and very much alive.

"Oh Papa!"

I was in his arms before he could get up from his seat. Charles came running in from the kitchen, wriggling and whimpering his joy.

"I was so worried," I said to Papa.

"I could say the same thing."

I opened the clasp of the leather satchel and drew out the vocalizer. "I know I'm too late, but I did get it back for you. That's why they attacked you, they wanted to steal it. I only wish I'd made it home sooner...." I trailed off, because tears were sliding down my cheeks and my voice was threatening to break. I looked around our wonderful, familiar home and gulped, trying to keep my emotions under control. "Oh, Papa, what are we going to do?"

He took the vocalizer from my hand and held it up to examine it, turning it this way and that. "Funny thing is, my girl, the darned thing never worked."

My mouth gaped open, and I felt my stomach descend towards the floor. "You mean I went all that way for nothing?"

Papa smiled gently. "We need to have a conversation about your impulsiveness, my dear."

"Oh Papa, I'm so sorry I worried you for days over nothing. But that means—the house—will we have to leave?"

"That's the most astounding thing about all of this. When Mr. Tamm came by yesterday afternoon, and I told him you'd flown in your own airship to go retrieve it, he forgot all about the vocalizer.

It seems a Mr. Bell had already filed a patent for a communication device anyway. But strangely enough, Mr. Tamm wasn't bothered by that one bit. Suddenly, all he wanted to talk about was your invention."

I felt a surge of pleasure. "He did? What did you tell him?"

"All I could do was repeat the specifics Uncle Adolphus shared with me on Thursday. Theo, is it true you got the weight of the boiler down to under two hundred pounds?" His eyes shone with interest, and I pulled up a chair to sit beside him, taking Charles into my lap.

"That's empty weight. It holds eighteen to twenty gallons of water, so it's considerably more."

"And you're able to generate your own hydrogen with the other part of the device?"

"Yes." I smiled.

"How long did it take you to get to Chicago?"

The smile faded from my face. "I don't know. I lost Uncle Adolphus's pocket watch during the storm."

"That's a shame, but we'll get another one. One more suitable for a young lady inventor and pilot."

A young lady inventor, he'd said. And pilot. At long last he was taking me seriously. Happiness filled my heart to overflowing.

"Did you arrange to have your invention conveyed from Chicago to Cincinnati?" Papa asked.

"It's already here. A man is bringing it to the house."

"Excellent. We'll meet with Mr. Tamm tomorrow so you can demonstrate everything for him."

"Papa, Kestrel Two was wrecked. I'll need at least a few days to make repairs." I looked down at my borrowed dress and dirty shoes. "And it might be nice to take a bath."

Papa laughed, and the sound gladdened my heart. I stood and headed toward the kitchen.

"Wait," Papa said, "You've only been home five minutes. Where are you going?"

"To see Emmoline. I want to send a hamper of food to someone tonight."

"Ah, that would be the helpful young man that Uncle Adolphus mentioned, wouldn't it?"

"Yes. He's got some bad things in his past, but I've decided not to hold it against him."

"You're no doubt talking about his involvement with the Ruffians and Quigley."

I stepped back into the room, listening to what Papa had to say with interest.

"Your Uncle Adolphus and I straightened all that out with the police yesterday. You see, I knew Henry's father, Peter Thorne. He was a colleague and friend of mine before he died. We collaborated on several projects. That man did the best metal and wooden casework of anyone I've ever known, and he was a superb boilermaker and metalworker. It was such a shame when he and his wife and family fell victim to the epidemic."

"What? You mean he was telling the truth? He isn't just a low-born thief?"

Papa shook his head. "Far from it. When we sent the police to check on his grandmother, they found that the Ruffians were holding her hostage in order to ensure Henry would do their dirty work. She is quite ill, and they've taken her to the hospital."

"But Henry doesn't know that. He'll be walking right into the Ruffians unawares—who knows what they might do to him." Alarm and fear for Henry flooded through me.

"They won't be doing anything. The whole lot of them were rounded up and hauled off to jail. Kidnapping, blackmail, theft, and conspiracy are serious things."

"Still, Henry won't know where his grandmother is. He was still at the station when I saw him last. I have to go find him to tell him where she is." I crossed toward the door, but Papa reached out a hand to stop me.

"That's already been taken care of. One of the officers was sent to find him at the train station. He's likely with his grandmother already."

My arms fell loosely to my sides. I was relieved to have something go right for once. Maybe instead of sending Henry that hamper of food, I'd take it to him myself.

Papa's eyes twinkled. "You mean to say you believed you were crossing into the next two states in the company of a hardened criminal? Goodness gracious, Theodocia. That is very inappropriate."

"I don't think I ever believed it. He was just too nice to be a wicked man."

Papa burst out laughing, and I turned back toward the kitchen.

"One more thing," he said.

I paused there in the doorway, waiting.

"You've had an amazing adventure, but I should prefer that all this—fending off criminals and the first flight of your airship, not to mention young Mr. Thorne—be kept out of the newspapers."

"But Papa, you just don't understand how powerful a demand there will be if word of my successful journey spreads. Truly, it's in our best interests to talk to the papers. But don't feel bad. That's the way with so many inventors, people like you often have no business sense."

He smiled and shook his head, gazing at me fondly. "I'm so glad you're home."

"Me too, Papa, me too."

You'd think that I wouldn't have been able to sleep for all the excitement that night, but in truth, I slept like a log. And I needed my rest. In two or three days, the Kestrel would have to be shipshape and ready to take to the air again.

People always say that good things come to those who wait. You usually hear it from old busybodies who don't want to stop gabbing long enough to give you the tea and cookies they've promised you. But I think better things come to those who refuse to give up, even if what they were being stubborn about was the wrong thing the whole time.

"Come on, Charles, let's go tell Emmoline I'm home."

SNEAK PREVIEW OF THE VOODOO QUEEN

If you enjoyed *The Rooftop Inventor: The Adventures of Theodocia Hews Book 1*, here's a sneak peek of the next book in the series: *The Voodoo Queen: The Adventures of Theodocia Hews Book 2*.

PROLOGUE

Letters from Perrine

3 Avril, 1879

Chère Tante,

Man came to me today asking me for some rootwork to protect him from spirits he claims are a haunting him. Did a reading, but nothing came clear but a great, dark evil, looming large over son tête. So I'm asking you for some chicory—cured that way you do it—to give comfort and strengthen the charm I'm making for him. Maybe some dried chamberbitter too. I will bring you some good cornmeal for couche-couche. See you Mercredi.

Votre nièce dévouée,
Perrine

15 Avril, 1879
Ma Chère Tante,
Man I told you bout three times before came round yet again. This time he ask for gris gris, cause evil won't leave him alone. He says he feel it flying around his head most nights. Never had three of my rootwork bags go weak before—usually three can do the job. Told him I don't do gris gris. Perrine is voodoo queen because she helps people, never hurts them. But he begged, and I could see the big dark stain on him without even asking the spirits bout it.
I come over by your house in town Vendredi to talk, all right? Need a new idea for it.
Votre nièce dévouée,
Perrine

23 Avril, 1879
Ma Chère Tante,
That tip of alligator tail you gave me won't work. Man keep coming round all the time. Can smell the stink o' fear pouring off him fore he even gets on my stoop. He's taken to lurking around waiting for me in marché and I decided to send Didiane north with la soeur de mon amie Madame Robichaux. She can work for them a while until we sort this trouble out. Best she don't know why.
I told man he should speak to Jolie Jamet now for kind of help he ask. Hate to send a paying customer to her, she's been so mean to me. But maybe she can do to his bad spirits whatever she did to those husbands. I can do no more for him, and it will be good to get clear of him.
Votre nièce dévouée,
Perrine

31 Août, 1879
Ma Chère Tante,
I need to clear out of back a town and come sleep by your house in the country like we talked bout—at least for couple weeks. Been having that trouble too

long now. I'll get that man with the fast new steam boat to carry me there. Look for me in less than a week, maybe Dimanche. Need to finish some work first.

Grosses bises et merci,
Votre nièce Perrine

CHAPTER 1

"But isn't there *some* sort of party we could go to?"

"Not tonight," I said.

A pout turned down the corners of Lettie's mouth, and she picked at the edge of the lace doily on the table beside her chair. "There's just so much more to New York high society than there is here," she said.

"So you've said. You've only just arrived. I'm sure something will turn up. We could go to the zoo this afternoon if you'd like."

"A pack of monkeys and two grizzly bears don't really interest me." She flicked one perfect blonde curl aside and picked up the small doily from the side table and began to examine it.

"They have a hyena from Africa and a tiger from India now. And a talking crow."

"A talking crow! There's no such thing."

"I'm not lying, they do. Anyway, how would you know? Birds are hardly your area of expertise."

She shifted on her chair and tapped her foot impatiently. "I would have thought that you'd take the time to plan some social outings for me." A frown wrinkled her delicate brow, and she turned loose the doily she'd been torturing and dropped her hand dramatically into her lap.

My cousin Leticia Hews had only been in Cincinnati for two days, and already she was fraying my nerves. Lettie always put on big city airs—but this time seemed different—she seemed more difficult than usual.

I knew exactly what she thought of my hometown, and it made me wonder why she bothered to come visit. Although we were first cousins and only a week apart in age, we couldn't be less alike. Lettie likes parties and ladies' teas and operas. I like getting my hands dirty inventing things.

You might have heard of me. My name is Theodocia Hews, and I'm the one who invented the aetherigible, the personal conveyance that will revolutionize short distance daily travel. Of course, most people assume my father Orin Hews invented it, but it is not so. It really was me. The story has been in all the papers.

When we were younger, I could persuade Lettie to do all kinds of entertaining things, like hiding in a train for an impromptu trip to Louisville, or setting a mechanical frog to croak out his song under the preacher's pulpit in church. But now that we were older, she'd wised up and become much more cautious. The last time she'd visited, I had to work twice as hard to get the same level of entertainment out of her. That's not to say it couldn't be done. In some ways, I think I rather enjoyed the bigger challenge. But this summer, Lettie was acting different—more grown up—and I wasn't sure I liked it. At all.

"Theo," she purred, "let's go see what Henry is doing."

END NOTES

Still here? Since I'm a big fan of real life history, I can't resist including a few end notes about the contents of the book.

Of course, Cincinnati, Xenia, Dayton, Delta, and Toledo, Ohio are all real places you can find on a map, as are Richmond, Indiana, Indianapolis, Indiana, and Chicago, Illinois. However, as *The Rooftop Inventor* is a steampunk fantasy and a work of fiction, from time to time I take liberties with these locations, and also with some historic events. Here are some of the historical places and facts I've used as a jumping off point for Theo's imagined world.

What's real...

The Little Miami River does meander in a mostly north to south direction as it runs its course between Xenia, Ohio, and Cincinnati, Ohio, to where it empties into the Ohio River a little ways East of downtown Cincinnati.[1] I've been canoeing on several stretches of this scenic river, and it's always great fun.

The Greene County Courthouse at 45 North Detroit Street in Xenia, the one that Theo and Henry saw from the air, was a white stone building with four Greek columns and was built in 1843. It did exist, but was torn down and replaced in 1901 with the current handsome (and larger) Greene County Courthouse with a tall clock tower.[2] Today, the Greek columns from the old courthouse stand at the entryway of Woodland Cemetery in Xenia.[3]

The Xenia Railway passenger station was built in in 1854 was indeed located near the intersection of South Detroit Street and Miami Avenue.[4] Some of the old railway lines have been made over into bicycle trails today and I've ridden on them with my family.

There really were huge flocks of passenger pigeons in Ohio in the nineteenth century. When migrating, they sometimes numbered in the millions, and according to the Audubon Society "they were the most abundant bird in the United States." They were still populous in the mid-1800s until they suddenly went extinct through over hunting with the last one dying in the Cincinnati Zoo in 1914[5]—which sparked the national conservation movement. In 2014 I saw a stuffed specimen of a passenger pigeon in the Indiana State Museum which made me curious about these extinct birds.

Cholera epidemics were common in Cincinnati in the 1800s and killed thousands of people. A particularly bad cholera outbreak occurred in Cincinnati in 1866, which would account for Theo losing her mother. A crematory was built in Cincinnati in 1884, largely to handle surges in the numbers of deceased bodies due to the epidemics.[6] Cholera continued to be seen in the United States until the early 1900s when improved sanitation and chlorination of water came about.

German immigrants did flock to Cincinnati in the 1800s because Cincinnati was becoming a major U.S. pork-processing center at that time. Many Germans lived in the area known as Over-the-Rhine, which is where Findlay Market is located. These are real places, still in existence today.[7]

The National road is real. Running east and west, work was begun in 1811 to connect Cumberland, Maryland, to Wheeling, Virginia (now West Virginia). The stretch of road from Springfield, Ohio to Vandalia, Illinois was completed in 1841. The roadbed was made of layers of stone called macadam. The National Road still exists today and is known as U.S. 40.[8]

Carbolic acid (also known as phenol) was indeed a powerful antiseptic used to clean wounds. British surgeon Joseph Lister pioneered its use in 1867. It's a good thing Theo didn't have any to use on Henry, because if it isn't properly diluted, it discolors the skin white, and further contact may result in burns that can be severe.⁹

The Great Chicago Fire was a real event that began on October 8, 1871 leaving devastation in the central business district and residential areas that was almost four miles long and three fourths of a mile wide. Reconstruction began quickly and continued for twenty-five years. Individuals, corporations, and cities from all around the United States sent monetary relief.¹⁰ And yes, Cincinnati was one of the cities that donated hundreds of thousands of dollars.¹¹

What's not real…

Tradition has it that Cincinnati, like Rome, was built on seven hills. Although these names are in dispute, according to one source these are: Mount Adams, Mount Auburn, Walnut Hills, Fairmount, Fairview Heights, Clifton Heights, and Price Hill.¹² While there is a real Belvedere Street in Cincinnati, Mount Belvedere is a fictional creation.

While John Jay was considered a founding father of the United States of America¹³ neither he nor the Continental Congress signed Emancipation into law during the Revolutionary War. I wish he had.

While there were five different inclines (or cable railways) built in the hills of Cincinnati between 1871 and 1892, with the Mount Adams Incline being the last to close in 1948, the Mount Belvedere Incline is purely fictional.¹⁴

The Indiana State Capital Building (also known as the Indiana Statehouse) is a real place in Indianapolis located on the old National Road, but I've fudged the dates so Theo could see this beautiful and massive landmark from the air. Planning did begin for the building in 1878, but the cornerstone wasn't laid until 1880, and construction wasn't completed until 1888.[15]

Regretfully, there never was an Aetherigible nor a Revolutionary Racing Steam Carriage, though I really wish there had been.

---

[1] Geology.com. Geoscience News and Information. Ohio Lakes, Rivers and Water Resources. Map. Accessed on April 12, 2015. http://geology.com/lakes-rivers-water/ohio.shtml.

[2] Xenia Area Chamber of Commerce website. Short History of Xenia. Accessed on April 12, 2015. http://www.xacc.com/staticpages/index.php?page=xenia-information.

[3] Woodland Cemetery website. Accessed on April 12, 2015. http://www.woodlandcemeteryxenia.com/.

[4] Greene County. Table, Stations of the Past. Station Name: Xenia, Little Miami RR. http://www.west2k.com/ohstations/greene.shtml.

[5] Yeoman, Barry. "Why the Passenger Pigeon Went Extinct." Audobon. May-June 2014. Accessed on: 5 March 2015. http://www.audubon.org/magazine/may-june-2014/why-passenger-pigeon-went-extinct.

[6] Prout, Don. Cemeteries. Greetings from Cincinnati. Accessed on 18 March 2015. http://www.cincinnativiews.net/cemeteries.htm.

[7] Ohio History Connection. German Ohioans. Accessed on April 12, 2015. http://www.ohiohistorycentral.org/w/German_Ohioans?rec=592.

[8] Harper, Glenn and Smith, Doug. "A Traveler's Guide to the Historic National Road in Ohio." Ohio National Road Association. 2010. Accessed on 5 March 2015.

http://www.ohionationalroad.org/TravelersGuide/TravelersGuide.pdf.

[9] WiseGEEK. Clear answers for common questions. What Is Carbolic Acid? Accessed on April 12, 2015. http://www.wisegeek.com/what-is-carbolic-acid.htm.

[10] Rayford, Jo Ann. Tragedy in the Chicago Fire and Triumph in the Architectural Response. Illinois Periodicals Online. Illinois History Teacher 1997, V. 4, No. 1. Accessed on 5 March 2015. http://www.lib.niu.edu/1997/iht419734.html.

[11] Lewinnek, Elaine. "Domestic and Respectable": Suburbanization and Social Control after the Great Chicago Fire. Iowa Research Online. 2003. Accessed on 5 March 2015. http://ir.uiowa.edu/cgi/viewcontent.cgi?article=1031&context=ijcs.

[12] City of Seven Hills. Cincinnati.com a Gannett Company. 4 December 2008. Accessed on 5 March 2015. http://archive.cincinnati.com/article/99999999/CINCI/81202017/City-seven-hills.

[13] USHistory.org. John Jay. The Declaration of Independence, Related Information. Accessed on 5 March 2015. http://www.ushistory.org/declaration/related/jay.htm.

[14] Prout, Don. Transportation. Streetcars, Inclines and Cable Cars. Greetings from Cincinnati. Accessed on 5 March 2015. http://www.cincinnativiews.net/cablecars%20inclines.htm.

[15] NPS.gov. National Park Service, U.S. Department of the Interior. Discover Our Shared Heritage Travel Itinerary, Indianapolis. Indiana Statehouse. http://www.nps.gov/nr/travel/indianapolis/indianastatehouse.htm.

A Note from Nooce Miller:

Thank you for buying this book.

If you enjoyed reading *The Rooftop Inventor*, please consider leaving a review wherever you buy or talk about books. Readers buy books because someone they know made a recommendation, and so in a way, I'm relying on you to spread the word about The Adventures of Theodocia Hews. Tell your friends, pester your local librarian, and write a review on Amazon. If you do, I'll be able to continue writing more books in the series.

And if you visit www.noocemiller.com to join my email list, you'll receive notifications and newsletters about upcoming books as well as access to special bonus materials. I'd also like to invite you to connect with me on Facebook (search for Nooce Miller) or on Twitter (my Twitter handle is @NooceMiller). I'd love to hear from you!

Again, it's your support that lets me keep on producing the entertainment you enjoy, so thank you for connecting.

May your steampunk dreams come true,

Nooce Miller

ABOUT THE AUTHOR

Nooce Miller began her writing career working as a technical and medical writer, but in spite of (or perhaps because of) that experience she has an enduring love for fantasy fiction. She enjoys traveling internationally with her husband and taking walks through her local woods and fields to experience the four glorious Midwestern seasons. She was born and raised in southwestern Ohio and currently resides in Indianapolis, Indiana.

Made in the USA
Lexington, KY
24 October 2016